Daughter of Storms

Louise Cooper

a division of Hodder Headline plc

First published in Great Britain in 1996 by Hodder Children's Books

10 9 8 7 6 5 4 3 2

A Catalogue record for this book is available from the British Library

ISBN 0 340 64070 7

Typeset by Phoenix Typesetting, Ilkley, West Yorkshire

Printed and bound in Great Britain by
Cox & Wyman Ltd, Reading, Berkshire

Hodder Children's Books
a division of Hodder Headline plc
338 Euston Road
London NW1 3BH

This story is for all my feline friends and acquaintances, past and present, including Candy, Dusty, Calidor, Asta, Oz, Jelly, Honey, Tom, Lionel, Tig, Timmy, Maeve, Miggins, Jess, Mitzi . . . and Bess, who sat beside me as I wrote and had her own (occasional) paw in it!

STAR PENINSULA
NORTHERN MOUNTAINS
SISTERHOOD COT
RUINS
FANAAN BAY
W. HIGH LAND PROVINCE
WESTERN SOUND
HANNIK
WESTER REACH
HAN PROVINCE
CHAUN PROVINCE
THE BRIG
N
NNE
NE
ENE
E
ESE
SE
SSE
S
SSW
SW
WSW
W
WNW
NW
NNW
CHAUN
S. CHAUN PROVINCE
SISTERHOOD COT
BYSSA
PROSPECT
C.A. SANDALL
©15.X.'95©

KENNET HEAD
EMPTY PROVINCE
SKAROCK
HAVENING
WKS
WHITESHOALS
EAST HAN PROVINCE
MELLEAN
WISHET PROVINCE
PORT SUMMER
SHU PROVINCE
SHU-KHADEK
This Map Compiled in the 183rd Year of the AGE of EQUILIBRIUM by the Chart Master in the High Margrave of SUMMER ISLE
LT. SHIP
WHITE ISLE

1

Shar Tillmer saw the first signs of the coming Warp from her window in the High Margrave's palace. It was nearly sunset, and Summer Isle was bathed in mellow light. But away to the north the sky was changing, its blue giving way to a flush of darkly ominous colours, and far in the distance she could hear the high, thin wailing that soon would rise to a shrieking cacophony as the supernatural storm came screaming in over the sea.

She shivered, partly with fear and partly with excitement. To watch a Warp was a terrifying experience but, unlike many people who dreaded their coming, she was exhilarated by them. After all, as her uncle Thel had told her many times, these great storms came from the realms of the gods themselves and were a sign that the seven lords of Chaos and the seven lords of Order watched over the world. And her uncle should know, for he had once been an adept of the Circle, and adepts were closer to the gods than any other mortals could ever hope to be.

But if Shar wasn't afraid, someone else was, and

she turned abruptly from the window as a small, faint whimpering sounded behind her.

The air elemental was crouching on her bed. It was a beautiful creature, like a fragile bird but with a mouselike head and huge amber eyes, and for the past hour Shar had been enjoying its antics as it darted playfully about the room. Now, though, its rainbow colours had dulled almost to grey and it was trembling.

'Hush!' Shar went to the bed and sat down, holding out a hand. 'There's nothing to fear; the storm won't hurt you.'

The elemental crept close to her – its touch felt like a butterfly's wing – and made the unhappy sound again. Shar tried once more to reassure it.

'Don't you understand the Warps? They're a sign from the gods, a good sign.' But the elemental only shuddered, and she reminded herself that for all its powers it was a simple creature, and in the low magical realm from which it came the gods and their deeds had no meaning. It was frightened, and that was all it knew.

'Very well, then.' Shar's eyes grew sympathetic. 'You needn't stay any longer. Go back to your own world – you'll feel safe there.'

She raised one hand and spoke the words of release. The elemental gave a sigh of relief, like a summer breeze. It rose into the air, hovered for a few moments, then winked out. As it vanished, the floor beneath Shar's feet vibrated slightly and outside there was a sudden livid green flash. The storm was getting closer and she went to the window again.

The sky was darkening rapidly. Huge, dim bands of colour were starting to wheel slowly across the heavens, and on the horizon lightning flickered like a silver net. The wailing was growing louder, accompanied now by a deeper rumbling, and though she knew she wasn't supposed to, Shar was tempted to open the window and lean out, to see and hear the better.

Her hand was almost, but not quite, on the catch when someone knocked at her door and a voice called her name.

Guiltily Shar jumped back, and her uncle came into the room.

'Watching the Warp?' Thel Starnor smiled, and the smile softened the contours of his severe face. 'Well, you're made of sterner stuff than most. But I think now you should close the shutters and go to bed. It'll be a long day tomorrow and we must all be up and about early.' He started to withdraw, then paused. 'Oh, and Shar – don't let too many of the cats in here tonight. The servants have been complaining about finding their hair everywhere.'

Shar's cheeks reddened, but Thel was grinning now and she knew that he didn't really mind. She crossed the room to kiss his cheek and said, 'Goodnight, Uncle.'

'Goodnight, my dear. Don't forget your prayers.'

He had said that to her every night since she was

three years old. Not that Shar would have dreamed of forgetting, for as a daughter of two Circle adepts and niece and ward of a third, she knew her duty to the gods. In fact, she decided, she would make her devotions now, before putting on her nightgown. That way she could leave the shutters open a while longer and the storm would be a fitting backdrop.

As her uncle closed the door behind him three small, sleek shapes had darted between his feet and through the gap, and now the cats came to wind themselves round Shar's legs, purring loudly. Why the palace cats were so fond of her she didn't know, but for as long as she could remember they had been her constant companions. According to Thel they had even been drawn to her when she was little more than a year old and he had first brought her here from the Star Peninsula far away in the north. Now the cats followed her wherever she went, sneaked into her room whenever they could, and on most nights at least two slept on her bed. They seemed to love her as much as the elementals did, and sometimes she could even pick up vague mental pictures from their telepathic minds. Cats didn't communicate very clearly with humans, but those who had psychic gifts could sometimes understand them. Shar knew she had such a gift. But it was as if the cats sensed something special in her. Something different.

'Now, all of you,' Shar said, 'I must make my prayers. Be still, and be respectful.'

The cats sprang on to her bed and sat down, gazing at her with their wide, mysterious eyes.

Outside, the sky had turned to the colour of a bruise and the lightning – green and crimson and blue and gold by turns – was almost continuous. The high wail of the Warp was like an eerie song in Shar's blood as she closed her eyes and spread her arms wide.

'Aeoris, greatest lord of Order; Yandros, greatest lord of Chaos; I offer you my homage at the ending of the day.' She knew the formal words by heart and recited them carefully, then added her more personal prayers for good fortune to the High Margrave, to her uncle and to her friends at the palace. And the cats, of course. Yandros, highest god of Chaos, would particularly understand her prayers for the cats. And lastly she offered prayers for her own mother and father, whom she did not remember but whose souls, she hoped, were in the gods' care. As she made that last prayer Shar's face clouded a little, and when the ritual was complete she sat down for a few minutes before her mirror, staring at her own reflection in the glass.

Auburn hair, cut to the shoulders, and hazel-green eyes. People said she was pretty, but Shar privately thought that her nose was too long and mouth too wide for her to have any hope of ever being beautiful. Had her mother been beautiful? Or her father handsome? What sort of people were they? For all that Thel had tried to tell her over the years, it was impossible to form an image of her parents' faces. If portraits of them had ever been painted they would be in the black castle on the Star Peninsula where Shar herself had been born. But that was in happier days, before her father died in an accident. And before her mother—

She stopped herself, not wanting to think about that. Five years ago, when he considered her old enough to understand, Thel had told her how her mother died, and it still hurt Shar to recall the unhappy story. Mad with grief, Thel said. Unable to bear the loss of her husband. And so one night she had walked through the black gates, to the edge of the huge pinnacle of rock on which the castle stood. From the rock there was a sheer drop to the sea. And Shar's mother had simply stepped over the brink.

Shar had been no more than a baby at the time, and Thel, her father's brother, was her only living relative. After their deaths he had officially adopted her, and soon afterwards he had resigned from the Circle and brought her here to Summer Isle, where he took up a post at the High Margrave's court. He hadn't returned to the Star Peninsula since, so Shar had never seen her parents' home, the home of the Circle sorcerers. One day she would go there. She had made a promise to herself a long time ago. And perhaps when that time came she might even be accepted as a candidate for the Circle itself, and follow where her father had led. *If* Thel could be persuaded . . .

Shar sighed. She was starting to feel unhappy, and that wouldn't do on the eve of the great celebration. Best to go to bed and sleep.

In the sky the wheel of the supernatural storm was

starting to turn faster and unearthly, ghostlike shapes flitted and danced across the wild sky. Shar looked up for a few moments, and in her mind another prayer formed. She knew she should give homage to the lords of Order and Chaos alike for they watched over the world equally. But, somehow, she had always felt a greater pull towards the gods of Chaos. Now she thought of Yandros of Chaos, and whispered, 'Great Yandros . . . please let my dreams come true.'

Yandros, of course, did not answer her. The gods never did. But she had spoken what was in her heart, and that was enough for her.

Shar reluctantly closed the shutters as the eldritch, howling voice of the Warp rang out over Summer Isle, and, with the three cats curling beside her, settled into her bed.

The storm passed before midnight and the day dawned bright and warm, with the strange, charged feeling in the air that Warps always left in their wake. Shar ate a quick breakfast and then hurried to prepare for the masque in which she was to take part. The masque was an entertainment of music, poetry and dance, to be performed on the palace lawns; Shar was one of seven 'Sea-Maidens' and had to recite a few solo lines. She was nervous, but everyone assured her that all would go well. Just as long as the cats didn't try to join in with her, as they had done at the final rehearsal.

To Shar's relief the cats kept away, and the masque went off perfectly. A great crowd watched it, sitting on the sloping grass bank in the west garden, and when it ended there was a storm of applause. The High Margrave, splendid in gold and crimson, made a speech thanking the players, then announced that music and dancing would begin on the north lawns immediately. This was the sign for everyone to relax, and Shar hurried away from the grass arena as quickly as she could. She wanted to mingle with the crowd – and she wanted to watch very carefully.

There were many distinguished visitors among the guests today. Province Margraves from the mainland, wealthy merchants and ship-owners, many women from the order of teachers and seers known as the Sisterhood who were easily recognisable in their formal white robes and silver headdresses. But Shar wasn't interested in them, for she had noticed something else. A large party of adepts from the Star Peninsula was here. She had seen them during the masque, men and women wearing the Circle's distinctive gold badges at their shoulders, and the sight of them quickened her pulse. For if she could speak to one of them, make herself known, it was just possible that she might learn something of her parents.

Thel's duties meant that he must stay with the High Margrave's entourage, and so Shar was, effectively, free to do as she pleased. The only difficulty was that without a formal introduction she didn't know how she could fall into conversation with the Circle initiates. Simply to walk up to them and present herself would be looked on as downright rude. How, then? She needed a convincing reason, an excuse for her forwardness. But the answer eluded her.

She was wrangling with the problem when the accident happened. A group of cats had followed her from the masque stage; she had shooed them away but two had ignored her order and were still trotting determinedly at her heels. Suddenly, for no apparent reason, one of them veered aside and dived between her feet. Shar stumbled, lost her balance, and with a startled yelp fell to the ground.

A feline face stared at her at eye-level, and the cat uttered a smug chirrup of satisfaction. Shar started to say a word that Thel would have disapproved of – then swallowed the curse hastily as she saw a pair of feet pointing towards her not three paces away.

The boy was perhaps a year or two older than she was, with a wind-tanned face and blond hair which he wore long in the northern style. Shar started to struggle to her knees with her dignity in disarray; he held out a hand and she took it, allowing him to help her to her feet.

'Your cat,' he said in an amused voice, 'has a peculiar sense of humour.'

'It isn't *my* cat.' Irritably Shar brushed grass from her skirt. 'The wretched creature was just following me. They always do.' Then, belatedly remembering her manners, she added, 'Thank you.'

But the boy wasn't interested in her thanks. 'They must read something in your mind that they like. At least, that's what my psychic-sense tutor believes.

We've a few people at the castle who have much the same effect on cats.'

Shar had been about to make an inconsequential reply, but the word 'castle' stopped her tongue. With a small shock she realised that pinned to the boy's coat was a gold seven-rayed star inside a circle. The combined symbols of Chaos and Order – the badge of a Circle initiate!

The boy made a quick, formal bow. 'Hestor Ennas, first rank at the Star Peninsula, at your service.'

So that was why the cat had done it. Shar glanced at the animal, which was now washing itself and pretending to ignore her, and suppressed a desire to laugh aloud.

'Shar Tillmer,' she replied, also bowing, 'who doesn't yet rank as anything at all. But my parents were both initiates of the Circle, and my uncle is a fifth-rank adept. He's retired now, and we live here on Summer Isle.'

Hestor grinned. 'Then I'd say that makes you as close to a true northerner as it's possible to be.' He paused. 'Can I get you some wine?'

It was an unorthodox introduction, Shar thought, and not quite what she had had in mind. Someone more senior would have suited her purpose better. But the cat had done its best to help her; and besides, she had taken an instinctive liking to Hestor. This might be just the beginning she needed.

'Yes,' she said. 'Thank you, Hestor. I'd like that.'

* * *

Within an hour Shar and Hestor were talking as if they were the oldest and best of friends, and their main topic of conversation was the Star Peninsula. Hestor's widowed mother was also an adept, and Hestor himself had been initiated into the Circle a year ago. Shar listened enraptured to his descriptions of their life at the castle, from the great and solemn formal ceremonies that honoured the gods to the smallest details of everyday events. She must have asked a hundred questions, eagerly absorbing Hestor's answers and storing them in her mind, before at last Hestor changed the subject and wanted to know more about her.

'What are your ambitions, Shar?' He indicated the scene around them. 'This is all fine and splendid, but I suspect you won't be content to be a courtier for the rest of your life.'

Shar's expression clouded a little, for though he didn't know it, Hestor had touched on a raw spot.

'My uncle,' she said carefully, 'wants me to join the Sisterhood. I seem to have a particular talent for working with elementals, you see, and so . . .' her voice tailed off and she shrugged.

'Elementals?' Hestor looked surprised. 'That's a skill better suited to the Circle, I'd have thought. The Sisters are fine when it comes to scrying and teaching, but elemental magic is the Circle's province.'

Shar looked into the distance. 'Probably,' she said non-committally.

Hestor regarded her for a few moments more. 'So

you really want to join the Circle, but your uncle won't permit it.'

She shrugged. 'He's an adept himself. He must know best.'

But her tone wasn't convincing, and Hestor said, 'Shar, listen. If your heart's really set on the Circle – and I can tell it is – then I could speak to my mother. She knows the High Initiate well, and—'

'Shar!' A voice interrupted from a short way off and they both swung round.

Thel was approaching. 'My dear,' he said, 'I've been looking for you everywhere. I wish to speak with you in private.' He paused, glancing at Hestor, then added in a faintly forbidding voice, 'I don't believe I know you, young man.'

Hestor bowed formally and introduced himself. Shar expected Thel to relax once he knew that Hestor was a Circle initiate, however junior, but to her surprise her uncle seemed displeased. After only the briefest of cool greetings he took Shar's arm and led her away, leaving Hestor staring after them.

'Uncle, what's wrong?' Shar asked as soon as they were out of earshot. 'Has Hestor offended you?'

'Of course not,' Thel replied brusquely.

'Then why are you annoyed?'

'I'm not annoyed, Shar.' Then he sighed. 'I overheard you and the boy talking about the Circle, and I'm simply disappointed. I've told you time and again that you must forget your hankering to be enrolled at the Star Peninsula until you're considerably older.'

'But Hestor has been initiated, and he's not much older than I am,' Shar pointed out.

'Maybe so, but it's different for those brought up at the castle. You know I want you to join the Sisterhood, at least for a few years. At a Sisterhood Cot you can learn to make the most of your talents, but you'll also be in surroundings that are more suitable for a girl of your age.' Thel stopped walking and turned to face her. 'I only want what's best for you, Shar. The Sisterhood *is* best – and if you parents were alive, I know they would take the same view.'

Shar was in no position to argue with that, and she felt guilty. 'I'm sorry, Uncle,' she said, then gave a helpless little shrug. 'It's just that I want so much to follow where Father and Mother – and you – have led.'

Thel's tone softened. 'I understand your feelings. And maybe one day in the future you'll have your wish. But for now, you must accept the settlement I've made for you.'

Shar started to nod, then abruptly stopped and stared at him. 'Settlement . . . ?'

'Yes.' Thel smiled. 'That's what I came to tell you. I've found you a place at a Cot where an old friend of mine, Sister Malia Bryse, is the Senior in charge. The final arrangements have just been agreed – and you are to leave Summer Isle the day after tomorrow.'

2

For Shar, it was as though a pall of cloud had blotted out the sun, spoiling the bright day and the celebration. One more day, just one, and she must say goodbye to home and friends and everything familiar, and embark on a new life.

It wasn't that she minded going away. After all, as a Circle candidate she would have had to leave Summer Isle. But that dream had been dashed – her uncle had made his decision and there was nothing she could do to change his mind.

She had tried to plead with Thel, begging for a little more time and secretly hoping that Hestor might meanwhile be able to speak to his mother as he had suggested. But Thel was adamant. Two Sisters from the Cot were attending the celebrations here on Summer Isle; when they left, Shar would travel with them. And that was that.

The only consolation for Shar was that Sister Malia Bryse's Cot was set among the mountains of West High Land. This was one of the most northerly of the mainland's ten provinces, and the Cot was less than a day's ride from the Star Peninsula itself. It was possible, Shar told herself, surely it was possible, that a visit to the castle might be arranged once she was settled. She said nothing of that to Thel but it helped to dispel the cloud of gloom a little.

She saw nothing more of Hestor. In fact it seemed that Thel was anxious to keep her away from all the visiting Circle adepts. Though she knew his motives were for the best, Shar couldn't help feeling faintly resentful. But perhaps, once she was at the Cot, she could send Hestor a letter by messenger-bird. And there might be the prospect of a visit . . .

Evening came at last, but as the sky turned crimson and the huge, burning ball of the sun began to set, the celebrations were still in full swing. Flamboys had been lit on the lawns, and the palace windows were ablaze with lanterns and torches. Then, as the sun touched the horizon, the palace's quartz walls caught the slanting light and the entire building seemed to glitter like something from a dream – or, as a visitor standing close to Shar said in an awed whisper, like a vision from the realms of the gods themselves.

Shar gazed at the shimmering palace but for once the beauty of the quartz's evening display didn't move her. Most of her friends had gone to join in the dancing and games on the north lawns; no one would notice if she slipped away to her room, and so with a sigh she headed for the formal gardens from where she could take a back staircase to the living quarters.

Where the flamboys were brightest a sparkle of tiny fire elementals, no bigger than bees, came dancing through the dusky air to meet her, and four cats and one half-grown kitten followed her. Shar felt a sharp pang at the thought that soon she must leave these small but dear friends behind, and she tried to project her sorrow to the cats' telepathic minds, hoping that they would understand. But they either couldn't or wouldn't see what was in her thoughts and only trotted silently at her heels.

Her bedroom was full of shadows and looked somehow very forlorn. Tomorrow she would have to pack . . . and suddenly, though she wanted to be alone, Shar didn't want to sit in the room with only her thoughts to distract her. Perhaps, instead, she would climb up to one of the palace's turrets. She would have a glorious view across Summer Isle as well as being able to watch the festivities from a distance, in peace and quiet. It might, after all, be her last chance.

The fire elementals had flittered away, not liking the gloom, and Shar retraced her steps to another staircase that wound up to one of the palace's highest towers. The cats came after her, but she was glad of their company for the stairwell was dark and the tower made her feel faintly uneasy. She passed doors, each leading to a room, but the rooms were disused and empty. One door latch rattled as she passed, making her jump before she realised that it was only the night breeze sighing in and stirring the air. She was over-imaginative; that was the trouble. There was no reason to be nervous.

Then Shar stopped, the hairs at the nape of her neck prickling as, suddenly, she heard something else. A shuffling ahead of her, as though someone had moved their feet. And what sounded like a faint cough.

She froze on the stairs. She could make out voices. Several voices, low-pitched as if people were whispering. They seemed to be coming from the floor above her and Shar moved slowly, cautiously, on up the stairs until she was level with the next closed door.

The whispering was louder. Shar paused, listening . . . and then she heard six clear words among the murmur:

'. . . *when we carry out the assassination*.'

A sensation of icy-coldness shot through Shar. For a few seconds the voices merged indistinctly again; then:

'. . . *the perfect time. Without it, the risk would have been too great. Such a high-ranking figure isn't an easy target* . . .'

It was a different voice this time, and Shar's heart started to pound against her ribs. What had she stumbled upon?

Then, suddenly and briefly clear among the mingling of voices, she heard a third person speak. The shock was so great that what he said didn't register in Shar's brain; she only stood rigid, mouth open, eyes wide, as recognition hit her.

It was her uncle's voice! There could be no doubt

of it; she knew him too well to make any mistake. Thel, among the plotters. Thel, a would-be assassin.

Shar spun round, her foot missing a cat's tail by a hair's-breadth, and plunged back down the stairs as horror and bewilderment boiled up like a tidal wave which threatened to overwhelm her. At the foot of the tower she turned and raced for the sanctuary of her room, where she flung herself face-down on the bed. The cats, which had followed, jumped on to the counterpane and gathered round her, mewing anxious enquiries, but Shar ignored them and lay among her pillows, staring blindly towards the open window and the star-filled night beyond. She couldn't believe it. It couldn't be true. It just *couldn't . . .*

Suddenly, fiercely, she sat up. This was ridiculous! Her uncle couldn't be an assassin. He had been an adept of the Circle, and now he was a high-ranking and trusted official at the High Margrave's own court. There had to be another explanation.

Then, with a new shock, she hit on a possible answer. Could Thel have discovered that a plot was in the wind, and was he acting as a spy, infiltrating the plotters' circle to gather enough evidence to expose them? Knowing her uncle as she did, she felt it made sense. And the alternative didn't bear thinking about.

Shar knew that she would have no peace of mind unless she could find out the truth. But that would be far from easy – she could hardly go back to the tower, knock on the door, and ask to be told!

Outside, light flared suddenly and a cry of delight went up from the crowds on the north lawns. Some apprentices from the Guild of Alchemists had prepared fireworks to add to the entertainments, and as green, gold and blue sparks showered into the air Shar remembered the fire elementals dancing around the blazing flamboys. This was the answer! An elemental – not of fire but of air – could enter the tower undetected, listen to what was being said and report back to her.

Shar scrambled to her feet and stood in the middle of the room, spreading her arms wide. Air; closing her eyes, she imagined open skies, whirling winds, and in her thoughts she reached out to her elemental friends in their strange, inhuman dimension. *Come to me*, she called silently. *Little ones of the air, I need your help – come to me now!*

Three times she repeated the call, then opened her eyes. For a few moments nothing happened. Then, abruptly, a sharp breeze blew in through the window. It skittered around the room and Shar felt a sensation like a cold breath on her face. One of the cats flattened its ears and hissed; then the elemental became visible, hovering above Shar's head. Silver and ghostly, its wings and fanned tail were a flickering blur as it gazed down at her. Shar sensed its curiosity and she held up one hand, beckoning. The creature spiralled down and settled on her outstretched fingers, and she whispered urgent instructions to it, praying that it would understand and be willing to obey.

Elementals were often unreliable, but it seemed that this time all was well for as soon as Shar finished speaking the creature rose into the air again and darted towards the window.

She sat down on her bed to await its return. The cats gathered round her; realising something was wrong they tried to reassure her with purrs and comforting telepathic images, but Shar was too keyed-up and nervous to concentrate. Time seemed to crawl by while the fireworks continued outside . . . then at last the elemental reappeared.

She knew at once that it had failed for its silver colour had dulled and it was very agitated. Urgently, she asked it what had happened.

A voice like a tiny, faraway bell answered her. 'There is power,' the elemental said. 'There is magic. I cannot go in; it is forbidden for any of us to go in.' It made a distressed sound. 'I tried. I tried . . .'

Shar understood. The plotters must have placed a magical protection around the tower, to ensure that no one could scry into their secrets. That could mean only one thing – that the would-be assassins had a sorcerer among their number.

The elemental was quivering unhappily, shaken by the repelling power it had encountered. Shar dismissed it with thanks and reassurances, and as it vanished back to its own realm she clasped her hands tightly together, her thoughts racing.

As a former Circle adept her uncle was a skilled sorcerer, and there was an old saying which ran,

'A thief can be caught by one of his own kind'. But Thel was running a great risk. If the plotters should suspect that he was deceiving them, Shar was certain they would have no hesitation in killing him.

Then a small, unpleasant inner voice said: But what if you're wrong, Shar? What if you're wrong, and he is one of the plotters?

Shar sat very still. She knew her uncle too well to believe that he could ever commit a terrible crime like this. And yet . . . dare she ignore the possibility that she had misjudged him?

The plan that had been forming in Shar's mind abruptly collapsed. She had resolved to speak to her uncle and beg him to tell her the truth, but now she realised that, until and unless she was absolutely certain about him, she must say nothing. In fact she must say nothing to anyone, for whom could she trust? Anyone in the palace could be involved.

Well, then, if she couldn't ask for human help, that left the gods themselves. But Shar knew that long ago, when the era known as the Age of Equilibrium dawned, the gods had promised not to take a direct hand in human affairs. Only the world's three rulers – the High Margrave, the High Initiate of the Circle and the Matriarch of the Sisterhood – had the right to call on them to do so. Shar had no such right, and to plead directly with Yandros and Aeoris would greatly anger the gods.

Shar tried to think clearly. She had stumbled on something of deadly importance, and somehow she must find a way to investigate further. Here on Summer Isle, or in the Sisterhood Cot at West High Land; it made no difference. She had other friends after all; the elementals would do what they could for her. There was a way to unravel this mystery. And, one way or another, Shar was determined to find it.

3

'Shar!' A hand shook her shoulder. 'Shar, wake up. We're almost there.'

Shar opened her eyes to see Sister Ilase leaning over her. The daylight was fading and the interior of the carriage was gloomy; outside she thought it was raining but couldn't be sure.

She blinked and sat up. It was hard to believe that the journey was nearly over; they seemed to have been travelling for ever. First there had been the seven-hour voyage from Summer Isle to the mainland, landing at the bustling port of Shu-Nhadek, capital of Shu Province. They had stayed in Shu-Nhadek overnight, then in the morning the private Sisterhood carriage had been waiting to carry them out of the town on to the main drove road and away towards West High Land. For the next ten days they had travelled steadily northwards, and though to begin with Shar had found the journey exciting, it wasn't long before the novelty wore off. Her two travelling companions were dull; Sister Ilase was elderly and prim, and Sister Corra, though much younger, hardly had a word to say. So Shar had spent much of her time sleeping as comfortably as she could on the carriage's narrow seat, with the beat of the horses' hooves and the whirr of the wheels sounding endlessly in her ears.

Then early this morning they had entered the pass that led through the northern mountains. They had an armed escort now, to protect them against the brigands who preyed on unwary travellers, and as dusk began to fall the escort leaders had lit torches to show the way. Shar lifted the curtain aside and peered out, but the pass was steeped in gloom and she could see only the flicker of the torches' flames reflecting from towering rock walls.

Suddenly she felt very depressed at the thought of all she had left behind on Summer Isle. Leaving the cats had been especially hard because they didn't understand that she was not coming back to them. Two dozen or more had gathered at the harbour to watch the ship sail away, and the sight of their tiny forms was more heart-wrenching than the figure of her uncle waving from the dockside.

And her uncle was another problem, for Shar had set sail with her dilemma still unresolved. She had spoken to no one of what she had overheard in the tower, and had not dared to use the elementals again. But she couldn't let matters rest as they were. She *had* to do something.

A shout sounded ahead of them, and suddenly they turned sharply on to a narrower track that led off the pass road. Echoes rang from the surrounding rock; for a few more minutes they clattered on – and then the mountains opened out into a valley, and Shar saw her new home.

The Sisterhood Cot nestled in the valley and was made up of several low, white buildings surrounded by a stone wall. Lights shone in many of the windows, and between the buildings Shar could see the shadowy outlines of a well-tended garden. The carriage began to descend, the horses going carefully on the winding path. Sister Ilase made a fuss of tidying Shar's hair, and within a short time they were pulling to a halt outside the Cot gates.

The gates swung open as Shar stepped down from the carriage. Wind and rain whisked in her face, carrying a scent of the sea, and she felt a huge pang of homesickness. But then, as white-clad figures emerged from the gate to greet them, she heard a familiar and welcome sound. With a loud and eager miaow, a ginger cat wriggled between the legs of two approaching Sisters and ran straight to her, tail raised high.. As she bent to stroke the purring creature, Shar felt some of her uncertainty slip away. Whatever the future might hold for her here, however lonely she might be among human strangers, she had already found one friend. And that was a good beginning.

Shar settled quite quickly into her new life. To begin with it was confusing as she tried to memorise the layout of the Cot and the daily routines of the

Sisters, but within a few days the white buildings were becoming almost as familiar as her home on Summer Isle. She had a room of her own, small but pleasantly furnished, in the Novices' wing near the refectory, and, provided she kept to her study hours and completed the chores allotted to her, she could do as she pleased within the Cot walls. She was even growing used to wearing the plain white Sisterhood robe with the Novices' gauzy veil to cover her hair.

The ginger cat was almost constantly at her side now, and Shar had been delighted to discover that the Cot had quite a colony of the small creatures. They all took to her, as animals always did, but the ginger became her firm favourite and she named him Amber because of his colour.

Her studies began on the day after her arrival. She was to learn the arts of scrying and divination, how to prepare and use healing herbs, and, surprisingly, the skills of elemental magic. Shar hadn't expected that, for, as Hestor had said, elemental magic was practised by the Circle rather than the Sisterhood. But her talent, it seemed, was looked on as something special. And it soon became clear to Shar that Sister Malia Bryse was taking a particular interest in her.

Shar had disliked Sister Malia on sight. She couldn't explain why, for Malia was a pleasant-faced, plump woman who seemed kindly enough. But something made Shar very wary of her. The cats seemed to avoid Sister Malia, and that, Shar thought, was a sure sign that something wasn't quite right. Then, within seven days, her unease grew into something stronger . . .

Shar had asked Sister Malia for permission to send two letters by messenger-bird. The first was to her uncle, which presented no problems. But the second, to Hestor Ennas, was another matter.

'A friend at the Star Peninsula?' Sister Malia pursed her mouth. 'Well, I don't know, Shar. Who is this friend?'

A little reluctantly Shar told her of how she and Hestor had met on Summer Isle, and said – a white lie, but she pushed her conscience down – that they had promised to keep in touch.

Sister Malia listened, then replied, 'No, child. I don't think it would be a good idea for you to exchange letters with this boy.' She smiled, but her pale blue eyes were suddenly cold. 'Messenger-birds are very expensive to use.'

'I'll gladly pay the fee from my allowance, Sister,' Shar persisted.

'You would only be wasting your money. The boy has his own studies and his own life to concentrate on; he's probably forgotten all about you by now.'

Shar knew that Hestor would have done no such thing, but before she could say so Sister Malia went on, 'Besides, I would prefer you not to start making friends at the castle. The Circle's methods of training are very different to ours, and I don't want your mind being confused or distracted.'

'But Sister—' Shar began.

She was interrupted. 'Shar, I don't need to remind you, do I, that a Novice in the Sisterhood is expected to obey her seniors without argument?' Sister Malia gave another and less pleasant little smile. 'No, I see I don't. So we'll hear no more about this matter. However, as you have made a promise, I will allow you to write one brief letter to the boy explaining that your studies don't allow you time for diversions. Present the letter to me for approval this evening.'

So in her room, with Amber sitting on her lap and patting the pen, Shar wrote to Hestor. She couldn't express her real feelings – the fact that Sister Malia was going to read the letter rankled – but hoped Hestor would realise from her stilted tone that she was doing what she was told rather than what she wanted. She took the letter to Sister Malia's office, stood silent while it was read, and received a nod of approval.

'This is suitable enough. I'll send it by the next courier.' Malia looked up. 'You may go.'

Shar went, feeling ruffled. Amber was waiting for her outside; they set off along the corridor together but suddenly the cat stopped, looked back at the office door and flattened his ears.

'Amber, what is it?' Shar asked in surprise. Amber took no notice; instead he hissed loudly, as though he had sensed something unpleasant. Shar tried to pick up the message in his mind, but the picture he gave her was too vague and jumbled to make any sense. All she knew for certain was that Amber was angry. But she didn't know why.

Until the following morning, when she collided with the servant girl in a doorway . . .

Sister Malia's office was tidied each day, and the servant was carrying her waste basket towards the refuse heap when Shar bumped into her. The basket dropped and a flurry of paper scraps scattered in all directions. Apologising, Shar bent to help the girl gather them; she scrabbled up a handful . . . and paused as, on one torn fragment, she saw familiar writing.

It was a piece of her letter to Hestor. And when she searched among the debris, Shar found others. Her letter, torn up and thrown away.

'Excuse me, Sister-Novice,' the servant said, 'but is anything wrong?'

Shar realised that she had been staring at the scraps of paper as if in a trance. Quickly she shoved the torn pieces into the pocket of her robe and said, 'No – I was – just thinking of something else.' They finished picking up the rubbish and Shar's face was grim as she watched the girl hurry away. So that was what Amber had sensed last night. He knew that as soon as Shar left the office Sister Malia had ripped up her letter. She had never intended to send it. So why had she told Shar a lie?

Back in her room Shar drew the torn pieces from her pocket to look at them again. As she spread them out she realised that by mistake she had picked up something else as well – a single sheet of paper, whole but folded into a tight little wad. Sister Malia's writing was on it, and Shar was about to throw it away when one word caught her eye. Her own name.

Her heart gave a peculiar lurch of shock, almost like a premonition, and she unfolded the paper. It seemed to be part of a letter; the ink had smudged so Sister Malia must have thrown this page away and rewritten it. Shar began to read. And what she read brought a crawling tingle to her skin.

'. . . to assure you that I am taking the greatest care,' the page began. 'Shar is watched, and I make sure that she has no contact with the outside world. Thus far this has presented no problems, and of course she knows only what she has been told, so . . .' A smudge blotted out the next few words and, seething with frustration, Shar skipped on. '. . . waited and planned for so long that we must make no mistake now. I understand that the arrangements made at the castle are as expected, and N . . .'

But there was no more, for at this point ink had spattered from Sister Malia's pen and she had discarded the page altogether.

Shar's pulse felt heavy, almost painful, as she read the words again. *She knows only what she has been told.* What, then, had she not been told? What secret was being kept from her – and why?

Shar would have given everything she possessed to see the rest of Sister Malia's letter. That, of course, was impossible – but if she couldn't read it she might at least find out where it was to be sent. Sister Amobrel was in charge of the Cot's messenger-birds; she would know if any were going out today.

Shar found Amobrel in the mews where the birds were kept, and as always the tall, jovial Sister was ready to chat.

'Today?' she said in answer to Shar's question. 'Yes, we've two birds with letters to carry. One to Wishet Province and the other to Summer Isle.' She smiled. 'Why do you want to know?'

'I . . . ah . . . I wrote to my uncle yesterday, and Sister Malia said she'd put my letter with her next package to Summer Isle. So I just wondered . . .'

'Oh, I see. Well, there is a package from Sister Malia, and it is going to Summer Isle. So your letter will be away this afternoon.' Amobrel gave her a conspiratorial grin. 'Don't tell me – you're asking your uncle to increase your allowance, and you're impatient for a reply!'

Shar returned the grin, hoping it was convincing. 'Something like that,' she said. 'Thank you, Sister Amobrel.'

So, then: Sister Malia had written to someone on Summer Isle. Surely, Shar thought, the letter could only be to her uncle. And in a dark part of her mind an awful suspicion began to form. Thel had told her that he and Sister Malia were very old friends, but now it seemed they might be more than that, for clearly they were keeping some secret between them. What had the fragment said? . . . *waited and planned for so long that we must make no mistake now.* Waited and planned for what? And suddenly a chilling thought came to Shar.

Could it be that there was some connection between this mystery and the assassins' plot? On the surface the idea seemed far-fetched. But a sharp, nagging intuition was working at the back of her mind – and she trusted her intuition. If there was a connection, then the smudged letter made it shockingly clear that in some mysterious way Shar herself was being used in the plan. And there was a connection with someone or something at the castle. That, Shar thought, unnerved, could explain why Malia had secretly torn up her letter to Hestor.

She pored over the fragment again, cursing the blot that had obscured the last word. What was 'N'? The beginning of someone's name? And: *the arrangements made at the castle are as expected*. Frustration boiled as Shar realised she couldn't hope to find answers by merely thinking. She needed help if she was to unravel this tangle of intrigue. And her best hope lay in her own special talents.

Over the next two days she made her plans. She was certain now that Sister Malia *was* watching her. Even outside study hours the Senior always seemed to be in the same vicinity as Shar. But Shar pretended to notice nothing untoward, and at last, on a wet, dismal evening, she was ready.

The items she needed had been easy enough to get. A small bowl, a pitcher of water, a piece of sealing wax; none of these would arouse suspicion. When the evening meal was over and the communal prayers to the gods had been said, she hurried back through the rain to her room, where Amber was waiting for her. Her door had no lock, only a latch, so Shar projected a telepathic message to the cat, asking him to stand guard and warn her if anyone should approach. Hoping he understood, she doused her lamp and sat down at her table to begin.

She hadn't attempted to call on her elemental friends since arriving at the Cot. The rain might help to attract them, but would they be willing to help her?

Thunder grumbled somewhere over the mountains as Shar poured water from the pitcher into the bowl and crouched over it, concentrating hard. In her mind she formed images of water – cascading falls, surging sea, flowing rivers – and softly she whispered words of summoning, of cajoling, of pleading. 'Help me. Please come to me now. Help your friend Shar . . .'

There was a strange little sound, like a faraway splash, and the water in the bowl rippled. Eagerly, Shar bent closer over the bowl. There was a faint glow coming in at the window from the refectory lamps, enough for her to glimpse a vague, shimmering shape below the water's surface, and the flick of a tiny, fish-like tail. The elementals had answered her call.

Shar cupped her hands round the bowl and deepened her concentration. In magical teachings, she knew, the beings of water were closely connected with dreams, and in dreams the answers to questions could often be found. Whether the elementals would send her a true dream tonight she didn't know, but she asked with all her heart for the answers she craved to be revealed to her. Then she lit a taper and held it and the piece of sealing-wax over the bowl. The wax melted and began to drip, and slowly and carefully Shar formed the letter 'N' in wax globules on the surface of the water.

'That is all I know,' she whispered softly. 'Please, if you can, tell me what it means. Reveal the truth to me in my dreams tonight!'

The water rippled again, but the floating wax letter kept its form. Was that a good omen? Shar couldn't say. But she thanked the elementals, then spoke the words that would release them back to their own strange world.

Outside, the rain seemed to have stopped. Shar rose to her feet, then picked up the bowl of water and slid it carefully under her bed. She felt light-headed and ready to sleep, so she called softly to Amber, telling him all was well, and climbed beneath her blankets. With the cat purring beside her she stared into the near-darkness for a few minutes. Then, praying that sleep would come quickly, she closed her eyes.

* * *

In her dreams, Shar saw a man. She had never met him but she knew his face immediately, for his portrait hung in the great audience-hall of the High Margrave's palace. He was standing with his arms upraised and he seemed to be speaking, though she couldn't hear his words. Then other figures swam into view around him; dark, hooded shapes, their faces hidden from view. Suddenly Shar felt an overwhelming sense of evil. Something was about to happen – she knew the man was in danger and she tried to call out, to warn him, but found she could make no sound. Then an appalling noise filled the air and in horror she looked up. Something vast and black was towering into the sky above her, a huge, shapeless darkness that roared like thunder. She saw it rush down on the man, heard him scream in agony, and suddenly her own voice broke free from its prison in a shriek of uncontrollable terror.

And the last thing she saw before she woke was the laughing face of Sister Malia.

Shar sat bolt upright in the early light of morning, hugging herself. Amber was on the floor, tail lashing and ears laid back; he had picked up a glimpse of the dream from her mind, but Shar was too stunned to comfort him. She had her answer. And it horrified her.

She scrambled out of bed. The bowl of water – she must look at the bowl of water! With fumbling hands she drew it out and her eyes widened as she stared at it.

The wax globules had floated apart and then reformed, this time into a complete word. Or rather, a name: Neryon. Shar knew that name. Indeed, everyone in the world knew it very well. And something else had happened to the wax. Last night it had been reddish-brown in colour, but that had changed. Now it was purple. And purple was the colour of death and mourning.

Shar's teeth began to chatter and a feeling of dread so deep that it was like a physical pain flooded through her. The elementals had sent her a true dream, for they had shown her who the assassins' target was to be. The plotters meant to murder a man who, after the High Margrave himself, was the most powerful and important figure in the entire world.

Their quarry was Neryon Voss, the High Initiate of the Circle.

4

Dawn was just breaking over the Star Peninsula when the air elemental skimmed out of the mountains. On ghostly wings it hovered over the headland, gazing at the huge landscape below. The morning was clear and windy – the elemental liked that – and under the red light of the early sun the spectacular coastline of the far north stretched away to east and west.

For a few minutes the elemental danced on the buffeting air currents, enjoying a game of its own. Then it remembered the mission it had promised to carry out. It didn't like the idea of being enclosed within the great castle, but the memory of its human friend's anxious face and desperate pleading was stronger than the dislike, so it swooped out across the peninsula and began to drift downwards.

The stack of rock on which the castle was built towered above the sea and was joined to the mainland cliffs by a rock bridge. The castle itself was no less spectacular – black as a moonless night, it stood square and solid and forbidding, dominated by four titanic spires at the four corners, like jagged fingers pointing towards the sky. The central courtyard was deserted and steeped in shadow and the creature cast about for the human it had been told to find. Ah – there, on the north side. He was still sleeping. But there was an open window . . .

Watched only by a curious cat down below in the courtyard, the elemental skimmed towards its goal. And at the Sisterhood Cot in the mountains, Shar lay awake in her bed, fists clenched, praying with all her strength she could muster that her plan would work. She had not dared to try to send a letter in secret; Sister Malia watched her too closely for that to be possible. So the elementals were her one hope of getting word to the High Initiate, to warn him of the danger he was in. And in the castle was the one person who could help her.

Hestor woke up with a start to find what felt like a gale howling through his bedroom. The curtains at his window were fluttering wildly, the rug on the floor flapping, and as he sat up in surprise the wind knocked over a water glass on his bedside table. The glass fell to the floor and smashed. Hestor scrambled out of bed, hair whipping across his face and mouth open in shock.

Then, as suddenly as it had come, the wind vanished. The curtains, the rug and Hestor's hair all flopped limply once more, and Hestor's eyes widened as he saw, hovering by the window, a pale, spectral shape.

An air elemental – but whatever was it doing here?

He hadn't yet learned to conjure elementals, and his mother had performed no magical work last night. Wondering if someone was playing a practical joke on him Hestor tried to remember the words of Binding that would force the being to tell him who had sent it. But before he could recall them a thin, whistling and gusty voice whisked through the room.

'Help me, Hestor! There is trouble! I am your friend. There is trouble! Tell Neryon Voss!'

Hestor hadn't the least idea what the elemental was talking about but its words alarmed him. 'What do you mean?' he asked it. 'What trouble?'

'Neryon Voss!' the elemental repeated. 'Neryon Voss!'

Hestor was baffled. If this was a message for the High Initiate, why was the elemental trying to give it to someone as unimportant as himself? Yet it hadn't made a mistake, for it had addressed him by name. He didn't understand!

The elemental was still repeating its words, growing more and more agitated, when abruptly another voice intervened.

'Hestor, whatever is going on? I heard you from next door – good gods, what's that creature doing here?'

Pellis Bradow Ennas, Hestor's mother, had emerged from her own room and now stood in the doorway with an astonished expression on her face.

'Mother!' Hestor motioned towards the elemental. 'It came into my room and it's trying to give me a message! But it's garbled – I can't make any sense of it!'

As a fifth-rank adept of the Circle, Pellis knew exactly how to deal with such a situation, and she stepped quickly forward to stand before the elemental. Her voice quiet and reassuring, she calmed it and then firmly told it to speak again, more coherently this time. What Hestor heard then made his spine tingle.

'I have come from Shar. Shar is my friend. She is at the Cot in West High Land and she has made a discovery. There is trouble; there is danger. Danger for Neryon Voss. I know this is true. My cousins of fire and water and earth know it is true. Hestor is Shar's friend. Shar has sent me to Hestor because he can help her. I am helping Shar because she is my friend. Shar is afraid.'

'What is the danger?' asked Hestor's mother.

'I do not know. I cannot say. Shar knows. Shar sent me to Hestor.'

Hestor said in alarm, 'Is Shar in trouble?'

'I do not know. I only know there is danger for Neryon Voss. That is all.' A pause. 'I do not like it here. This place is too small. I do not want to stay.'

'Very well,' Pellis told it. 'You have been kind; I thank you. You may go.' And she spoke the releasing words.

With a sigh of relief that set the curtains fluttering again the elemental vanished, and Hestor and Pellis turned to look at each other.

'Mother,' said Hestor, 'we can't ignore this.'

Pellis frowned. From what Hestor had told her about Shar, she didn't sound like the kind of girl who would play silly jokes. Besides, the elemental had been genuinely alarmed.

Hestor spoke up again. 'If Shar's at the West High Land Cot, I could reach it on horseback in less than a day—'

'Wait, Hestor,' she interrupted. 'I'm inclined to agree that we can't ignore this, but neither do I want you doing anything hasty. I'll think things over while I get dressed, then we'll have breakfast in the dining-hall together and talk about it.'

Hestor would have preferred to sort matters out then and there, but knew it was pointless to protest. His mother would make her judgement in her own good time, as she always did. His only consolation was the thought that her judgements, and the decisions that followed them, were usually wise.

The castle's huge dining-hall was crowded when they met there again half an hour later. Morning light streamed in at the tall windows, and the tables and benches that filled the hall were crowded with Circle adepts and their families. Pellis ordered bread, spiced cake and a hot fruit-cup for them both, then, lowering her voice, said, 'Hestor, I have little doubt that the elemental *was* sent by your friend Shar, and that its message was genuine. However, I don't think we should alert the High Initiate until we know more. It could be that there's some mistake or misunderstanding, and I don't want to worry

Neryon without good reason – especially with the double eclipse so close.'

Hestor had forgotten about the double eclipse; a very rare conjunction of both moons that was due to take place just before the summer Quarter-Day. The event was to be marked with a great deal of ceremony, and the High Initiate was already deeply involved in the preparations. 'Of course,' he said. 'Then, Mother, what about my suggestion? That I go to the Cot, see Shar for myself and find out what's going on?'

'I'm not sure. The mountain passes aren't safe, and—'

'I could take an armed servant with me. Please, Mother – we obviously can't write to Shar and ask her what she's discovered, because that might put her at risk. So this is the only way!'

Pellis looked at her son. She was foolish to worry about him, she told herself. He wasn't a child any more but almost a young man. And he was obviously deeply worried about his friend.

'We-ell . . .' she said uncertainly.

'Thank you, Mother!' Hestor jumped up from the table and gave her a great hug that squeezed all the air from her lungs. When she could breathe again Pellis laughed. 'You're just like your father; you can always talk me round! Very well, then. You may go. But I want you to be very careful.' Her brow creased. 'I don't know why, but I have an uneasy instinct about this.'

Hestor hid his jubilation behind a sober expression. 'Don't worry,' he said. 'I won't take any chances.'

When Hestor and Pellis left the dining-hall, a solitary figure at the next table watched them go. They had taken no notice of him; he was simply another Circle adept taking breakfast. But the gaze that followed them was steel-hard, and the mind behind the gaze was deep in thought. The boy and his mother had spoken in low voices, but nonetheless the watcher had overheard much of what they said.

He finished his own meal and then left the hall. In his private room, with the door locked, he sat down and wrote an urgent letter. And when the letter was finished and sealed, he took it to the falconer's quarters with orders for a special messenger-bird to be sent to Sister Malia Bryse.

The adept returned to his room. He knew Sister Malia would do whatever needed to be done at the Cot, but that still left the problem of Hestor. They could afford to take no chances. So it would be as well to make further plans.

Hestor left the castle at dawn the next morning with a burly servant whose name was Ranil. The servant carried a long-bladed sword and two knives, while Hestor was armed with a smaller sword. Even the youngest initiates were trained in the use of weapons, and on a journey like this, through brigand country, it was wise to be well armed.

They crossed the dizzying bridge from the castle stack and were soon riding through the mountain pass. Hestor tried to make conversation but Ranil didn't seem to want to talk. At length Hestor gave up his efforts and they rode on with only the echoing noise of the horses' hooves to accompany them. At noon they stopped to feed themselves and their mounts. Then, with the sun high and its rays slanting down into the canyons, they resumed their journey. Barring accidents, Hestor calculated, they should reach the Cot by nightfall.

It was mid-afternoon when it happened. They were in a particularly narrow section of the pass, Hestor riding in the lead while Ranil followed close behind. A scattering of stones made Hestor turn round – just in time to see Ranil raise his sword and swing it at his unprotected back.

Hestor gave a cry of astonishment, and the sound of it made Ranil's horse swerve in fright. The point of the sword whistled past, missing Hestor's arm by a hairsbreadth. In the sudden confusion Hestor saw that the servant's face was twisted into a mask of pure malice.

'Ranil!' Hestor shouted. 'What in the name of the gods are you *doing*?' But Ranil only spurred his horse forward again, and the sword came up for a second time.

Hestor didn't know why the man had tried to attack him – but he did know that he was in terrible danger for Ranil was a skilled swordsman with a longer and heavier blade. And the ice-cold look in his eyes left Hestor in no doubt of his intentions.

'Ranil, I don't understand this! Why—'

Ranil interrupted him with a sneer. 'Save your breath for your last prayers, boy.'

'Kill me, and you'll go to the block for it!'

'There are enough brigands in these mountains. They'll take the blame, and a dead brat can't tell tales!'

Hestor's heart was pounding and his mouth was so dry that he felt he might choke. Ranil was staring at him like a snake hypnotising its prey, and Hestor's hand shook on the hilt of his blade. If he could just get it free without the man noticing . . . He couldn't hope to beat Ranil in a sword-fight, but there might be another way. It was a terrifyingly slim chance, but the only one he had.

Ranil had begun to smile now, a cruel, chilly smile. 'Last prayers, boy,' he said again, mockingly. 'I'll give you to the count of fourteen, and then—'

He got no further, for suddenly Hestor's sword had come free and with the speed of sheer desperation he swung it up and aimed, not at Ranil, but at Ranil's horse – a wild blow with the flat of the blade, catching the animal stingingly across the withers. The horse whinnied and reared high, forelegs raking the air, and with a yell of surprise Ranil pitched backwards out of the saddle.

Hestor didn't wait to see him hit the ground. Wrenching his own horse round he urged it into a gallop and they were away along the track, a cloud of dust kicking up in their wake. As he crouched over the animal's neck Hestor heard other hoofbeats behind them as Ranil's riderless mount bolted, but he didn't slacken his pace. He knew he had escaped death by a hair's-breadth – but mixed in with the fright was fury. For Hestor was certain that Ranil had no personal grudge against him, and nor had he suddenly gone mad. Someone had known the purpose of this mission. And that same someone had paid Ranil to ensure that the mission would not be carried out. To Hestor, that could only mean one thing. The elemental's warning had been all too real.

Ranil's runaway horse was slowing down and falling behind. It didn't matter; even if Ranil caught it again Hestor knew he had too good a start for the servant to overtake him. Nontheless he spurred his own horse on harder. There was no time to lose now. He had to reach the Cot and find Shar. For, now that one attack had failed, their enemies might strike a second time – and Shar would be an all-too-easy target!

5

Hestor arrived at the Cot at sunset. His weary horse was taken to the stables, and anxious Sisters hurried Hestor away to the refectory to give him a hot meal. They were horrified to hear the story of Ranil's treachery – such a dreadful thing, and a castle servant, too! – and said that Sister Malia must be told at once.

Sister Malia was told, and as Hestor finished his meal she came to see him. Hestor took one look at her face, and in the moment before she masked it he saw the truth in her expression. She, like the Sisters, was horrified. But her horror had a very different cause. Sister Malia had been warned that he was coming here. And she had not expected him to arrive.

However, she made a show of outrage and sympathy. She promised to send a message immediately to the High Initiate, a promise which Hestor suspected wouldn't be kept, and said that he must stay at the Cot until he recovered from his ordeal, when she would provide him with a proper escort back to the Star Peninsula. Hestor had a shrewd idea of what that would mean, but he pretended to be grateful.

Then he asked to see Shar.

'Shar?' Sister Malia didn't so much as blink. 'I'm afraid that isn't possible.' A smile, but her eyes were suddenly cold. 'Shar is unwell.'

'Unwell?' Hestor echoed, alarmed.

'Yes. A summer fever – not serious, but it is virulent.'

'It came on very suddenly this morning,' one of the younger Sisters volunteered. 'Poor Shar. I expect it's the change of climate; she isn't yet used to our colder weather.'

Dismayed, but determined not to be put off, Hestor said, 'Couldn't I see her just for a few minutes? I shan't tire her.'

'I'm sorry, but no,' Sister Malia repeated. 'The fever is contagious, and she must stay in isolation until it passes.' Her look became sterner. 'The High Initiate would not be pleased if you caught the illness and carried it back to the castle. I will pass on any message you wish to give to Shar, but I can't permit you to visit her.'

Hestor thought he detected just a hint of gleeful malice in her voice. He didn't argue . . . but he had his own ideas about the fever. Chances were that Shar wasn't truly ill at all. Chances were that she had been drugged.

Satisfied that Hestor wouldn't make trouble, Sister Malia left, instructing that he should be shown to a guest room. For a moment Hestor wondered if he would be safe, but then dismissed his doubts. In the mountains it would have been easy to do away with him and make it look like a brigand attack, but here in the Cot it was another matter. If any harm came to him under her own roof, Sister Malia wouldn't be able to explain it away. He was safe enough.

But that still left the problem of getting to see Shar. Hestor decided to wait until after second moonset. By that time even Sister Malia was sure to be asleep, and if he could find out where Shar's room was it should be easy enough to sneak in without anyone knowing.

In his room he blew out his candle and sat down to wait. It was hard to stay awake, and once or twice he almost dozed off, but by pinching himself and splashing his face several times with cold water, he managed to keep sleep at bay.

At last the second moon dropped behind the mountains and the Cot was silent and still. Luckily Hestor's room was on the ground floor, so rather than go through the corridors he opened the window and climbed out into the cool night air. The novices' quarters were on the far side, past the stable block; he had heard one of the Sisters say so. Better not risk going straight across the courtyard; he'd keep to the wall and make his way round.

Finally he reached the building he wanted and stopped, narrowing his eyes in the dark to peer at the line of windows in the long wall. The windows had shutters, but at this time of year they were left open at night. One set of shutters, however, was closed.

Hestor smiled in the dark. Shar was in isolation, to stop the 'fever' from spreading. So this must be her room. He tiptoed to the window and slid back the shutter bolts. They eased open with only a small creak, and Hestor fumbled for the frame of the glass underneath.

Suddenly, startling him so that he nearly yelped aloud, the window was pushed open from inside. In one awful moment Hestor knew that he couldn't duck down in time. He froze – and from inside the room Shar stared back at him.

'They locked me in,' Shar said. 'So I knew something was afoot. But I didn't dream it would be you, Hestor! I didn't *dream* you'd come here!'

She had told him her whole story, including the truth about the 'fever'. Early this morning Sister Malia had sent for her to discuss some new lessons and she had had breakfast in the Senior's study instead of the refectory. Suspecting nothing, Shar had eaten the food. An hour later, she collapsed.

'I slept all day,' she said, 'and when I woke up this evening I felt perfectly all right. But the door was locked. That was what made me suspicious. Then Sister Malia came – she said I had a fever, and I must stay in bed and have no visitors. She brought me a bowl of broth and told me to eat it all. I knew there was nothing wrong with me, so when she had gone I poured the broth away.'

Hestor had no doubt that the broth, too, had been drugged, 'Sister Malia knew I was coming,' he said. 'Someone must have warned her.'

'Someone at the castle? But who?'

'I don't know.' The trouble was, Hestor thought, there were so many possibilities. Anyone might have found out about his journey and destination. 'But it proves one thing,' he went on. 'Your dream was right. Whatever's going on, Sister Malia *is* involved in it.'

Shar shivered. They hadn't dared to light a candle in her room and the darkness suddenly seemed menacing. 'Hestor, what can I do?' she whispered. 'I feel so helpless! And if I try to call on the elementals again—'

'That's too dangerous!' Hestor interrupted. 'If you tried, and Sister Malia found out, the gods alone know what might happen! Anyway, she'll be watching you even more closely after this. No; there's only one thing we *can* do. We must go back to the castle – both of us – and tell Neryon Voss everything!'

Shar's eyes lit. 'You mean escape? Tonight?'

'Yes. Whatever she might suspect, Sister Malia won't expect us to act so quickly. So by the time she finds us gone, we'll be well on our way. It's our only hope, Shar.'

Shar nodded. 'All right. We'll have to steal a horse for me. Go to the stables, Hestor, There's a back way out that leads straight on to grass, so we can get away silently. I'll change my clothes and meet you there.'

Ten minutes later they were leading Hestor's chestnut gelding and a grey mare out through a small gate in the wall, away from the main entrance. The escape was so easy that Hestor could hardly believe they had succeeded; only when they were on the mountain track, and he looked back at the Cot undisturbed and silent in the valley behind them, did he finally allow himself to breathe freely.

They set off as fast as was safe in the darkness. Sunrise was about three hours away; if they didn't press the horses too hard they should be able to keep going until noon, then rest for an hour or two before continuing. Shar on her grey mare looked like a ghost in the night; she kept glancing over her shoulder as though expecting to see someone – or something – following them. Nothing did, however, and the only sound was the rhythmic thudding of hooves and creak and jingle of harness as they hastened on.

At last a first faint glimmer of light showed on the high peaks above them. Hestor gave silent thanks to the gods that they had come safely through the night, but just as he did so, he heard a noise among the rocks ahead.

'Shar . . .' He reined in quickly and Shar, alarmed, did the same.

'What is it?' she hissed.

'I'm not sure.' Hestor was peering into the gloom to where the track curved sharply. 'I heard something. It might be an animal, but—'

He broke off as a shower of small pebbles came tumbling down the slope ahead. Above them, on a ledge, shadows moved abruptly.

'Shar, ride!' Hestor shouted, an awful intuition taking hold of him. 'For your life – GO!'

Shar dug her heels into the mare's sides and the horses sprang forward. There was a yell from overhead, and suddenly a dozen or more dark shapes erupted from the shelter of the rocks, leaping down the sheer drop on to the track. Shar saw savage faces, burly forms, the flash of knife-blades; then a figure hurled itself at her, grabbing for the bridle. With a cry she kicked out. Her foot caught her attacker full in the face but her horse was out of control in the middle of the uproar. *Brigands!* Shar screamed Hestor's name but she couldn't see him in the mêlée and the darkness and it was all she could do to cling to the saddle and not be hurled down among the trampling feet and hooves. Then she heard the clash of metal and knew Hestor was fighting for his life – for both their lives, for she had no weapon to defend herself. They were hopelessly outnumbered. Now two more men were rushing at her. She tried to wrench her horse out of their path but a sword flickered in the murk, the tip of the blade cutting a shallow gash in the grey's flank. The horse jackknifed into a wild, kicking leap, barging the men aside, and for a moment they were clear of the struggle. Through the flying curtain of her hair Shar glimpsed Hestor battling against four assailants, and suddenly, violently, her instinct reacted. Hardly knowing what she was doing, she shrieked at the top of her voice, 'Help us, friends of air and fire! *Help us*!'

The frenzied scene seemed to twist before her eyes. She felt a surge of energy from her own mind – and the air around her erupted. Searing heat and shattering cold hit her like physical blows, and tongues of fire burst into life above her head, streaming in a ferocious wind, as a host of elementals appeared.

'Save Hestor!' Shar cried. 'Help Hestor!'

A blue fireball spitting lightning whirled towards the brigands. With cries of astonishment they fell back – but then from the ledge above a new voice roared out in a tongue Shar didn't understand. A bolt of darkness hit the fireball and it exploded, shattering into useless fragments. The wind, too, collapsed and scattered, and Shar heard the elementals' thin, high-pitched shrieks as they were beaten back by a wave of power. Someone was using sorcery against them! This was no ordinary attack!

Terror rose in her mind. She had failed; the elementals couldn't help them, couldn't save them, she and Hestor were going to die—

'*Hestor*!' she screamed, '*Hestor! Oh gods! Oh Yandros of Chaos*—'

Her cry clashed with the noise of the elementals and the shouts and triumphant laughter of their attackers as they surged in for the kill. Shar opened her mouth to scream to the gods again—

And her voice, together with every other sound, was eclipsed by a titanic howl from the sky.

Shar's mare reared and Shar was flung from the saddle. By a miracle she fell clear of danger, rolling against the rock wall, and as she scrabbled breathlessly to regain her feet, the canyon was plunged into mayhem.

A wave of churning darkness swept over the heavens and the howling swelled to a hurricane roar as the entire scene distorted into something out of nightmares. The brigands' cries changed to yowls of alarm, and as the mountains shook to the echo of the colossal noise from above, the shock of realisation hit Shar. Exploding out of nowhere, thundering down on them like the voices of the gods themselves, they were in the middle of a Warp storm!

A network of blood-red lightning split the sky, and in the brief, gory blaze of it she saw that the brigand attack had collapsed in turmoil. Men were running, panicking, covering their heads with their hands as they fled for shelter. More lightning flashed, a blinding bolt that turned night to day, and high overhead bands of grim colour were starting to march across the sky like the spokes of a vast, spectral wheel.

With a squeal of terror the grey mare bolted past Shar, knocking her back against the rocks. Gasping for air she looked wildly around. Where was Hestor?

In the confusion and the flickering light she couldn't see him, and though she tried to call out, her voice was dwarfed by the din of the supernatural storm.

Then she glimpsed him. He was on the ground but still hanging on to his horse's reins, struggling not to let the frantic animal escape. Stumbling, almost falling, Shar started towards him. '*Hestor*—' The Warp answered her with a renewed clamour like the shriek of damned souls. The ground shook under her feet, threw her off balance – she saw Hestor's face stark in a new blaze of lightning, looking upwards in shock.

Then came a gargantuan, blinding flash, and the world was blotted out.

6

Shar opened her eyes to find herself staring at a watery dawn sky. For a few seconds she lay still, wondering where she was. Then, abruptly, memory came back.

The Warp . . . With a jolt she sat upright, then winced as her head spun. But the dizziness cleared as she looked around. Though she was still in the mountains, this part of the road was completely unfamiliar.

Where was she? Shar began to scramble to her feet; then alarm gave way to relief as she saw Hestor. He too was lying on the ground, but he was beginning to stir and mutter. A few paces away his chestnut gelding grazed peacefully.

'Hestor!' Shar scrambled towards him and helped him to sit up. Hestor blinked owlishly at her, then shook his head.

'What happened?'

'The Warp struck us.' Shar started to feel his arms for broken bones. 'Are you hurt?'

'No . . . no, I'm all right.' A quick glance at her. 'You?'

'Only a bruise or two. But Hestor, something's happened to us. Look around.'

Hestor stared in dawning astonishment. 'Great Aeoris and Yandros! This isn't the same road!'

'That's what I thought. Where are we?'

'Wait . . . I think I recognise it.' He scrambled to his feet. 'In my saddlebag – there's a map.'

He fetched it and they pored over it together. The twists and turns of the road meant nothing to Shar, but suddenly Hestor stabbed a finger at the paper. 'There! I thought as much!' He turned and stared her, awed. 'Shar, we're on the same road, but much further north. We're less than an hour's ride from the Star Peninsula!'

She was astounded. '*How*?'

'The Warp, of course! Don't you remember the legend? That Warps have the power to transport people from one place to another?'

'Yes, but I've never heard of it actually happening to anyone! Or at least, not for centuries!'

Hestor nodded 'Not since Equilibrium. But before then there were all kinds of stories about Warps being sent directly by the gods to help or punish humans.' He shivered suddenly. 'Yet this . . . it's the only possible explanation, Shar. The Warp must have carried us here!'

Shar, too, shivered. And she remembered, in the moments before the supernatural storm had broken, her own despairing plea to Yandros of Chaos. Had Yandros heard her, and answered? Or had some other power – some power locked within her own mind – called the Warp to their aid?

Hestor was folding the map again. 'It's only just past dawn,' he said. 'My horse can carry us both, so if we—'

He stopped as a groan sounded from behind a nearby rock.

'Whatever—' Shar started to say, but Hestor shushed her. He moved soft-footed to the rock; she followed, and they both peered round.

A figure was lying prone on the ground. He was small and underfed, black-haired and dressed in clothes too big for him. On the back of his skull a long, shallow gash was oozing blood.

Hestor said softly, 'Great gods – it's one of the brigands!'

'But he's only a boy!' Shar stared in astonishment.

'Maybe, but he was with them – I saw him.' Hestor moved closer, then bent and turned the boy over. He groaned again and his eyelids fluttered. He was, Shar realised, a year or two younger than they were.

'He must have been injured in the panic,' Hestor said. 'And somehow when the Warp snatched us away it took him, too.'

The boy moaned and mumbled something. 'Quick!' Hestor added. 'He's coming round – have you got anything we can tie him with?'

Shar pulled off the belt of her dress and Hestor bound the boy's hands. As he finished, the boy's eyes opened. He saw them and made a convulsive movement to pull away, then said a word that made Shar's ears tingle.

'Enough of that! Hestor pulled him into a sitting position. 'What's your name?'

The boy stared from one to the other with a hostile blue gaze. 'What's it to you?'

'Quite a lot,' Hestor said, 'considering that you're one of the brigands who attacked us!'

'I'm not!' the boy protested; then his eyes shut. 'My head hurts. I think I'm going to be sick. . .'

He was, and as he doubled over, Shar saw with sudden pity that his back where the shirt had ridden up was marked with bruises and weals. She nudged Hestor, pointing, and when he too saw the marks he raised his eyebrows.

'Maybe there's more to him than meets the eye,' he said in a low voice. 'In which case, he might be quite eager to talk.'

He was right. When the boy recovered, he proved very willing indeed to answer Hestor's questions. His name, he said, was Kitto. He didn't know his clan name, or even if he had one; he had lived with the brigands for as long as he could remember and thought that their leader might be his father or uncle or cousin, though he wasn't sure and no one had ever bothered to tell him. No, he said in answer to Hestor's accusation, he wasn't proud of being an outlaw! He didn't like setting up ambushes, and hurting people! But what would *you* do, he demanded, if to disobey meant being beaten with a stick or a horsewhip? Sometimes he did try to refuse, and then – well, they'd seen his back for themselves, hadn't they?

Hestor asked him then about the attack, and Kitto shrugged. Yes, the brigands has been told what to do – and had been paid well to do it. They were to watch for a fair-haired boy and dark-haired girl riding northwards through the pass, and their instructions were very clear. The girl was to be captured unhurt. But the boy. . . Kitto shrugged again. The boy was to be killed. That was what they had been paid to do.

'Who paid you?' Hestor demanded.

A third shrug. 'Don't know.' Then Kitto looked up at him almost challengingly. 'But I overheard the men say it was someone at the castle.'

'At the—' Shar began, shocked, but Hestor interrupted.

'It makes sense.' His face became grim. 'I didn't tell you before, but when we were ambushed I saw Ranil among the men attacking us.'

'The servant?'

'Yes. So whoever paid Ranil must have paid the brigands, too. There's someone much more powerful than Sister Malia at the back of this, Shar. Remember what happened when the elementals tried to help us? It would take a skilled sorcerer to drive them back. Especially as he must have done it from a distance.'

Shar shivered. If Hestor was right, and someone at the castle was behind this plot, then by going to the Star Peninsula they would surely be heading into even more danger. But when she voiced her fears Hestor shook his head.

'We can't change our plans. These traitors won't dare try to hurt us right under the nose of the Circle. Anyway, we know that there are at least two people at the castle we can trust – my mother, and the High Initiate himself. We'll be safer there than anywhere else.' He looked thoughtfully at Kitto. 'And so will he.'

'Me?' Kitto said uneasily.

'Yes. You're coming with us – your story will help to convince the High Initiate. Besides, you don't want to go back to your brigand friends, do you?'

Kitto looked rebellious. 'I'm not going to that place!' he argued. 'I can look after myself. Just untie me, and – *uh*!'

As he spoke he had tried to get to his feet, but his right ankle gave way and he fell back, face contorted with pain. '*Rot it all to the Seven Hells!*'

Hestor smiled thinly. 'Twisted ankle? Well, you can't run away on that! Come on; the castle physicians will patch you up.'

Kitto didn't argue any more but suffered himself to be legged-up on to Hestor's gelding, and with Hestor holding the bridle the little party set off. Shar tried not to think about what lay ahead. Her dream of seeing the castle was about to come true, but not in any way she had imagined. She was afraid of what might await them. And at the back of her mind, nagging like a sore tooth, was the thought of her uncle. A skilled sorcerer. A one-time Circle adept. He wasn't a traitor, she told herself. He couldn't be . . .

But under that determined feeling was a growing doubt.

Shar was stunned by her first sight of the Star Peninsula. As they emerged from the mountain pass she could only stand awestruck, taking in the huge vista of the world's northern edge spread out before her. Beyond the coast the sea glittered like a vast, polished mirror in the morning sun – and directly ahead, across the rock bridge that linked the mainland to the stack, was the castle.

For a moment Shar's resolve almost failed her. The bridge looked so narrow; there was no rail, no parapet, and for a moment she thought wildly that she would rather face the brigands than this dizzying crossing. But Hestor was already leading the horse forward. To him, it seemed, the bridge was nothing, so Shar took a deep breath and made herself follow.

The walk over the bridge wasn't quite as bad as she had feared. Kitto, on the horse's back, had turned pale and shut his eyes, but Shar found that after the first few steps it was easy to pretend that she was on level ground rather than suspended over a dizzying drop to the sea. They reached the other side safely, but as they walked under the great black arch Shar's heart started to pound with another kind of fear. The castle looked so gloomy, so grim . . . even the mountains of West High Land were less bleak than this.

They emerged into the courtyard and her fears redoubled as she stared at the courtyard. The black walls towered on all sides, filled with windows from which it was only too easy to imagine countless faces staring down at her. In the courtyard's centre was a stone pool with a large, ornate fountain, but in the shadows of the walls even that looked ominous and unfriendly. Shar felt very small and vulnerable, and she began to wish that she hadn't embarked on this reckless quest.

But it was too late for regrets, for their arrival had been noticed and people were hurrying towards them. Someone helped Kitto to dismount, then a groom came to lead the horse away, and suddenly they were in the midst of a small crowd who all seemed to be talking at once. Where had Hestor been? What had happened to the black-haired boy? Who was Shar? Kitto, feebly protesting, had been carried away to the castle physician and Hestor was trying to evade the questions when a newcomer came on the scene. Shar had a dazed impression of a tall, brown-haired woman with kindly eyes, then, to her enormous relief, she heard Hestor say, 'Here's Mother!'

Pellis Bradow Ennas took charge immediately, and within a minute Shar was being led into the castle, up a wide, sweeping staircase and through a bewildering maze of passages to a large and comfortably furnished room. This, she realised, was the apartment where Hestor and his mother lived, and as the door closed she felt a surge of weary relief. Here, at last, they were safe – or as safe as they could be.

As Shar sank on to a couch, Hestor took his mother aside, speaking in a low, urgent voice. As Pellis listened her expression became grim, and when Hestor finished she said, 'Very well. Clearly this is serious, as you feared, and the High Initiate must be told. But before I speak to him, I would like a few words with Shar.' She smiled at the girl. 'You must be hungry and thirsty. Hestor will go to the dining-hall and fetch you some breakfast.'

Hestor knew that she wanted him out of the way for a few minutes and he nodded. When he had gone, Pellis sat down on the couch next to Shar and took hold of her hand.

'Shar, my dear,' she said gravely, 'Hestor has told me what happened to you both. Obviously you have your own story to add, but I must be sure of one thing.' Her eyes narrowed and she looked intently into Shar's face. 'I must be sure that what you say is the truth.'

Shar stared back at her, and felt a sharp, inward shiver as she realised that this was no ordinary scrutiny. As a high-ranking adept of the Circle, Pellis was skilled in sorcery and she was using that skill to judge whether or not Shar could be trusted. For one alarming moment Shar though she would shrink away, unable to meet the woman's steady and almost accusing gaze. But suddenly she thought: My father and mother were adepts, too. What would they think of me if they knew I'd failed my very first test? With an effort she stayed still, forcing herself not to blink, and after a few seconds Pellis relaxed.

'Very well,' she said, 'I see there's no deceit in your thoughts.'

'You can . . . read my mind?' Shar ventured nervously.

Pellis laughed. 'Oh, no, Shar, not at all! No one has that much power. But I can read something of your nature, and it's clear to me that you're a very honest girl.' The she smiled a warm and kindly smile. 'Added to what Hestor has said about you, that's good enough for me.'

Abruptly, Shar's doubts slid away. She liked Hestor's mother. She instinctively trusted her. And the relief she felt at having her for an ally was enormous. At last, she thought, she was among friends.

But then she remembered that that wasn't strictly true – for even under Pellis's protection, she still wasn't completely safe. Someone here was in league with the assassins; someone with sorcerous power. Shar and Hestor had no idea who that person might be.

But the unknown enemy knew them . . .

7

Shar and Hestor were summoned to the High Initiate's study at noon. Pellis went with them, and though she assured Shar that there was nothing to fear, the prospect of standing before Neryon Voss in person made Shar's legs turn weak.

She tried not to show her nervousness as they reached the study and Pellis knocked at the door. At least, she told herself, she looked presentable, for Pellis had found her some fresh clothes to wear and she had also ventured down to the wonderful seawater pools in the castle foundations, where she had enjoyed a luxurious bath.

A voice from inside the study called, 'Enter,' and they went in. The High Initiate was sitting at his desk, by a window which let a stream of sunlight into the room. The desk was cluttered with papers, and Shar was surprised to see that the room was very untidy. Somehow she had expected the High Initiate to be extremely well organised, and the fact that he wasn't lessened her terrors a little.

Neryon Voss stood up. He wasn't as tall as she had imagined, and he was also quite young, which surprised her. He had light brown hair, hazel eyes and a pleasant face, and his clothes were very ordinary; just a simple shirt and trousers. The only sign of his rank was the gold badge pinned at his shoulder; a seven-rayed star inside a circle, the combined symbols of Chaos and Order.

Neryon nodded to Hestor, who made a formal bow, then his gaze turned to Shar. 'And this is Shar Tillmer?'

Shar bowed in the way that Sister Malia had taught her, but she didn't have the courage to speak.

'Shar; Hestor,' the High Initiate said. 'I understand from Pellis that you two have had some alarming adventures.' He looked from one to the other of them, and his eyes narrowed slightly. 'I think you'd better tell me the whole story from the beginning.'

Shar was hesitant at first, but Hestor encouraged her to speak freely, and they told the High Initiate all they knew. Neryon questioned Shar closely about the conversation she had overheard in the tower on Summer Isle, and also seemed very interested in her conjuration of the water elementals. At last the tale was finished and, as Shar and Hestor fell silent, Neryon sat back in his chair. His face was thoughtful.

'Well,' he said, 'there seems little doubt that something is afoot. What you overheard on Summer Isle was real enough, and so was the attack in the mountains. But as for the rest . . .' He looked hard at Shar. 'Elementals are often unreliable, and the water beings could have been mistaken, or even playing a trick on you. There's no real evidence to suggest that I am the plotters' target, or that Sister Malia Bryse is a potential assassin. And the idea that your uncle could be involved – I simply don't believe that. Thel Starnor is an old and good friend of mine.'

Shar bit her lip and said nothing. Neryon continued.

'Nonetheless, I will investigate this further. And, for a while at least, you had better stay here at the castle. I'll write to Sister Malia' – Shar opened her mouth but Hestor nudged her warningly and she bit her protest back – 'to let her know you're safe, and I'll put you in Pellis's care.' He smiled wearily at Hestor's mother. 'That is, if Pellis doesn't mind?'

'Not at all, High Initiate,' Pellis said.

'Good. Oh, and the boy Kitto – he may stay too. I've heard his story and I think he deserves a chance to make a better life for himself.' Neryon Voss nodded to them both. 'Very well, then. You may go.'

Dazed, Shar let Hestor steer her out of the study. Pellis had stayed behind with the High Initiate, and as the door closed Shar sighed heavily.

'He doesn't believe us,' she said.

'Oh, I think he does,' Hestor countered. 'If he's already talked to Kitto, he must be taking this seriously!' Then seeing that Shar wasn't convinced, he added, 'I'll take any wager he's telling Mother now what he really thinks.' A grin. 'And Mother will tell me. I'll persuade her.'

* * *

Shar was given a room of her own, close to Hestor and Pellis's apartments, but though she was made welcome she still found it hard to settle at the castle. She knew that the High Initiate had now written to Sister Malia, and the thought of how the Senior would react made her very uneasy. And underlying that was the fear, which she couldn't shake off, that even here she and Hestor weren't entirely safe. The unknown traitor at the castle had already made two attacks on them. There was sure to be a third, but how, and when? She felt so vulnerable knowing that she could do no more than watch and wait.

To make matters worse the investigation wouldn't begin for some time yet, for the High Initiate was too busy preparing for the double eclipse of the moons that was soon to take place.

Hestor had told Shar about the eclipse, adding that as well as being a rare event it was also potentially very dangerous. Everyone knew, of course, that the sun was sacred to Order and the moons to Chaos, and since the Age of Equilibrium began the lords of Order had watched over the world during daylight hours, while the lords of Chaos kept it safe through the night. However, with the sun vanished and both moons eclipsed, the protective powers of both Order and Chaos would be lost. As an old saying put it, the eyes of the gods would be blinded. And dark powers from other dimensions – demons and monstrosities which the gods' influence normally kept at bay – would be free to prey on the mortal world and on human souls. It was therefore the duty of the Circle to perform a great ceremony that would hold back these evil influences until the eclipse passed and 'the eyes of the gods' could see once more. The rites were complicated and difficult; Neryon, as High Initiate, would have the most demanding part to play, and until the eclipse was over he simply wouldn't have the time or energy to spare for anything else.

To ease the worry and frustration she felt, Shar tried to distract herself. She would have liked to explore the castle more fully, getting to know its maze of passages and stairways, but the place's brooding atmosphere and a more rational fear of the unknown enemy within its walls stopped her. With Hestor often at his studies she would have felt very lonely and vulnerable . . . but help came from two quarters.

Firstly, of course, there were the castle's cats. Within a day they had recognised a kindred spirit, and soon they were following Shar in twos and threes wherever she went. And secondly, to Shar's surprise, there was Kitto.

Kitto's ankle was on the mend, and once he had got over his first terror of the castle and realised that he wasn't about to be imprisoned as a brigand, he set out to make friends of both Shar and Hestor. Kitto had no wish to return to his old life as an outlaw, and he was determined to make himself so useful that he would be allowed to stay at the castle for good. Rather like the cats, he took to following Shar around when Hestor was studying, and with someone to accompany her she was less dubious about exploring the castle.

Which was how she discovered the library, and the answer to a question that had troubled her all her life.

The library was reached by a small door in the courtyard, opening on to a spiral staircase that wound down into the castle vaults. It was a large room, lined with tall shelves and filled with tables and benches; lamps burned in brackets on the walls and the air was filled with a dry, dusty, papery smell. Kitto, who couldn't read or write, would have shrugged his shoulders and started straight back up the stairs again, but Shar was fascinated, and as there was no one else in the library she began to look idly through the shelves. And on one shelf, in a row of old leather-bound books, she found the records of Circle adepts past and present.

Shar's heart thumped with excitement, for in addition to personal details about each adept, the records contained sketches of their faces. Quickly she thumbed through the pages, hoping, hoping – and suddenly before her were two faces, and two achingly familiar names, Solas and Giria Tillmer Starnor – her own parents.

Kitto heard the sharp little sound she made, and turned round to see her eyes filling with tears. 'Shar?' he said. 'What's the matter?'

Shar swallowed. 'I-I've found pictures,' she replied

unsteadily. 'Look Kitto . . . I've found drawings of my mother and father.'

Kitto had heard the story of Shar's parents and his face was sympathetic as he came to look over her shoulder.

'Your mother was pretty,' he said, then ventured a smile. 'You look just like her.'

Shar managed a watery smile in return but said nothing, and Kitto pointed to what was written beneath the sketches. 'What do all those words mean?'

She shook her head. 'They don't say much. Just when they were born, and when they married, and the dates of their initiations into the Circle.' It was all so impersonal, she thought. It told her nothing about them. And that made her ache inside.

Tentatively, Kitto asked, 'Is there anything about when they . . . well, you know . . .' He didn't like to say the word 'died'.

'No.' Shar had already looked. 'No, there's nothing at all.'

Kitto frowned. 'That's a bit strange, isn't it?'

That hadn't occurred to Shar before, and she turned the page, wondering if perhaps the record continued. But it didn't; there was only a new entry for another adept. No mention whatever was made of her parents' deaths.

'If I was keeping these records,' Kitto said, 'I wouldn't leave out anything as important as that. Would you?'

Shar bit her lip. 'No, I wouldn't.'

'You ought to talk to Hestor's mother,' Kitto continued. 'After all, she must have known them quite well. She might be able to tell you more – that is, if you really do want to find out.'

There was a pause. Then Shar said, 'Yes . . . yes, I do.' There was something strange about this, she thought. Thel had always been cautious when talking about her parents, as if there was more to their story than he wanted to tell her. Now it seemed that the castle-dwellers, too, were keeping something hidden. Shar wanted to know more. Hestor's mother would surely agree that she of all people had a right to know.

With gentle fingers she traced the outline of her mother's face on the paper. 'You're right, Kitto,' she said. 'I'll ask Pellis.' Then abruptly she closed the book with a snap and put it back on the shelf. 'Come on. I don't want to stay down here any longer.' A shiver shook her, which she tried to hide but Kitto saw. 'This room's too full of other people's memories.'

Shar was silent as they made their way back up the stairs and across the courtyard to the castle's main wing. Kitto followed, wondering if he should have held his tongue, and three times he opened his mouth to say so before thinking better of it. They went through the double doors, and started to climb the wide staircase towards the living quarters.

They were halfway up when there were sounds of

footsteps in the hall below them, and an angry voice said, 'Shar!'

Shar froze, then turned round. Standing in the hall, hands on hips and a thunderous expression on his face, was Thel.

'Uncle . . .' Shar's cheeks turned white, then scarlet, then white again. 'What are you doing here?'

'I should have thought that was obvious, Shar! When I received Sister Malia's letter—'

'She wrote to you?' Shar was so horrified that she interrupted without thinking, and that only made Thel angrier.

'What else did you expect her to do in the wake of your stupid prank, girl? I am your guardian, and responsible for you! It was sheer good luck that I was in Han Province on business, and so was able to come straight to the castle. Now, you will kindly come down here at once, and explain what in the names of the fourteen gods you think you were doing!'

Several other people had appeared in the hall and were watching and listening with amused interest. Horribly embarrassed by the small audience, Shar started slowly down the stairs. But Kitto hung back, suddenly thoughtful. So this was Shar's uncle . . . how convenient that he should just happen to be in Han Province, much nearer to the Star Peninsula than to Summer Isle – and even more convenient that Sister Malia should have known it. Could he have been travelling north anyway? Kitto asked himself. As if he was already on his way to the castle? As if he had known Shar's whereabouts even before the High Initiate sent his letter to Sister Malia?

Shar had reached the foot of the stairs and Thel was talking to her in a low, furious voice. Kitto couldn't hear what he was saying, but he decided that Shar needed help. Quickly and quietly he turned and hurried on up the stairs in search of Hestor.

'I'm only sorry, Neryon, that you've been put to so much trouble.' Thel had calmed down now, but he still gave Shar a fierce look as he spoke. 'I will, of course, take Shar back to the Sisterhood Cot. And I trust this foolish escapade, or anything like it, will not be repeated!'

There were four of them in the High Initiate's study: Neryon himself, Thel and Shar, and Pellis, who had come at Kitto and Hestor's urging. Shar looked pleadingly at Pellis, but she was watching the High Initiate. And there was a small frown on her face . . .

Neryon said, 'Of course, Thel, as Shar's guardian you must do as you think fit. However, I would like Shar to stay on at the castle for a while.' He smiled. 'I gather that she has a rather unusual talent for working with elementals, and naturally that's of great interest to the Circle. If she—'

Thel interupted sharply. 'I think not, Neryon.' Then, as the High Initiate looked surprised, he hastily made his tone more pleasant. 'As you pointed out, I am her guardian, and it was my decision that she should join the Sisterhood rather than the Circle. Sister Malia is more than capable of giving her all the training she needs. She will return to the Cot.'

'Well, legally I can't argue with you,' Neryon said. 'But under the circumstances—'

'Under the circumstances, she deserves punishment rather than the castle's hospitality! But I'm prepared to overlook her misbehaviour, provided she obeys Sister Malia from now on. Besides,' Thel added, 'I mean no offence to Pellis, but I suspect her son is to blame for leading Shar astray.' Suddenly his eyes grew very hard. 'If I were High Initiate, Neryon, I would be strongly tempted to expel him from the Circle for his stupidity and recklessness.'

Pellis's mouth set in a tight line, and for the first time Neryon Voss looked angry. 'Then, Thel, it's Hestor's good fortune that you are not High Initiate,' he said with an edge to his voice.

'Indeed it is. Well, I think there's no more to be said. Shar and I will leave first thing tomorrow.'

'As you wish.' Then Neryon nodded to Shar. 'Very well, Shar. You may go.'

Shar fled, and Thel left the High Initiate's study a few minutes later. Pellis, however, stayed behind, and when Thel had gone she turned to the High Initiate.

'There's something strange about this, Neryon. Why is Thel so insistent that Shar should leave the castle?'

'I don't know,' Neryon said. 'But we have no choice other than to let her go. If she was a Circle initiate I could overrule him, but as things stand we have no rights over her.'

'Hmm.' Pellis's eyes narrowed. 'Could that be why Thel doesn't want her to join the Circle? Because he would lose his control over her?'

'It's possible, though by all the gods I can't imagine what difference it would make. She'll be of age in a few years anyway. Still . . .' Neryon paused. 'I didn't tell him the real reason why Hestor brought her here. He believes the whole thing was simply a piece of mischief, and I think that's just as well.'

'Do you suspect Thel *is* involved in this plot?' Pellis asked, shocked.

'No-o. I'm not saying that.' The High Initiate looked steadily at her. 'It's simply a precaution, Pellis. That's all.'

8

All thoughts of asking Pellis about her parents were pushed out of Shar's mind by the urgency of her new predicament. Hestor was horrified when she told him, and immediately started to think of ways in which Thel might be thwarted. Kitto had a few suggestions, too, but as these involved either running away again or, preferably, arranging for Thel to have an accident, no one took them seriously. It began to seem that nothing would save Shar from an enforced return to the Cot.

But then Hestor had the most reckless idea of all.

'It's called an Oath Ceremony,' he told Shar. 'And by performing it, you'll make a pledge to the gods which can't be broken. If your pledge is to stay at the castle, there'll be nothing Thel can do to make you leave. He won't dare go against a sacred promise like that.'

Shar's eyes lit up, then her look grew dubious. 'But can I do it?' she said. 'I'm not an initiate, I don't know the ritual.'

'I do, and I can teach you. It isn't complicated.

We'll have to wait until late tonight, of course, when no one will see us going to the Marble Hall—'

'The Marble Hall?' Shar echoed.

Hestor smiled. 'Of course; you've never seen it, have you? Normally it's only used for full Circle rites, but if we perform the Oath Ceremony there, it will give it extra significance.' He paused. 'First-rankers aren't supposed to go there without permission and someone older to supervise, but your safety is more important than rules, so I'm willing to take the risk. Are you?'

Shar had learned about the Marble Hall in her catechisms. A great chamber deep below the castle foundations, it was the most sacred place in the entire world, for it contained the gateway to many different dimensions . . . including the realms of the gods themselves. Risk or no risk, the thought of seeing the Marble Hall for herself, and of taking part in a ceremony there, thrilled her to the core of her soul and she said eagerly, 'Yes. I'm willing!'

The second moon was starting to set when Hestor came to Shar's room. Shar was awake; too keyed-up to sleep, she had been silently rehearsing the words of the ritual which Hestor had taught her. Two of the castle's cats were curled at the foot of her bed; they woke and wanted to follow but Shar gently pushed them back and, carrying a candle apiece, she and Hestor slipped out into the dark corridor.

The castle was eerily quiet. Faintly in the distance

Shar thought she could hear the roar of the sea, but there was no other sound to break the silence. They met no one in the shadow-haunted passages and soon reached the courtyard by a side door. As they crossed the flagstones Shar looked up at the huge, black spires towering into the night, and suppressed a nervous shiver.

'Come on,' Hestor whispered. 'We have to go through the library.'

The spiral staircase was like a murky well waiting to swallow them, and the candles cast ominous shadows that followed them all the way down. In the library Shar hugged herself and tried not to shiver as Hestor led her through the gloom to a small alcove in the far corner, all but hidden by shelves. She had never noticed this niche before, but in it was a low door, which Hestor opened. Dim grey light shone beyond the door, revealing a narrow and strangely symmetrical passage leading slightly downwards; they doused their candles and began to walk down the slope.

The glow grew stronger as they went on, until it was almost as bright as day. Then before them was another door, made of metal and shining with a weird, soft phosphorescence. This, Shar realised, was the source of the light, and she hung back a little as Hestor approached the door and laid a hand on it.

The door swung open. Hestor looked back over his shoulder and smiled. 'Come on,' he said.

Slowly, Shar moved forward, and stepped over the threshold of the Marble Hall.

The Hall was filled with a swirling mist of soft pastel light that curled and flowed through the air as though it were alive. Tall, slender pillars filled the Hall like a marble forest, and the walls and ceiling were invisible in the haze. Beneath her feet, the floor was a complicated and beautiful mosaic of pale colours, arranged in patterns that seemed to move and change as she looked at them.

Shar let out a soft, astonished breath. Legend had it, she knew, that the Marble Hall's dimensions were fractionally out of step with the normal laws of time and space. It was said to be impossible to touch its boundaries, and as she gazed wonderingly about her she felt dwarfed and insignificant.

Hestor said, with soft pride in his voice, 'Isn't it beautiful?'

'It's wonderful.' The word was completely inadequate but Shar couldn't express her feelings any better. What must it be like, she thought wistfully, to be an initiate of the Circle and to know and use this incredible place as they did? She would give anything, anything, to share that privilege.

Hestor led her across the mosaic floor. In the mist ahead darker shapes loomed suddenly, and Shar's eyes widened still further as she saw what they were. Seven statues, more than twice the height of a tall man, each one depicting two figures standing back to back . . . these were the only images in the world of the seven lords of Order and the seven lords of Chaos. Their stone faces gazed across the Marble Hall, and Shar, mesmerised, stared at the central and tallest statue, which depicted the two greatest gods, Yandros of Chaos and Aeoris of Order. Aeoris looked serene and stern and aloof, but Yandros's narrow mouth and slanting eyes had a hint of dark humour that she found disturbing and yet exhilarating at the same time. Tonight she would make a solemn pledge in their names, and the thought made her shiver.

Hestor, too, had stopped before the central statue, and he looked at Shar, his expression serious. 'Well?' he said. 'Are you ready?'

Shar nodded, and Hestor turned to face the figures of the gods. He made the splay-fingered sign of reverence to all fourteen deities, and Shar followed suit. Then Hestor spoke.

'Great Aeoris, master of the powers of Order; great Yandros, master of the powers of Chaos; I come to this place in reverence, and I speak with the rightful authority of a true initiate of the Circle.' He bowed to the statue. 'I bring to this place a candidate with a pledge to be heard and sanctioned so that no mortal power may oppose it.' Now he turned slowly on one heel until he was facing Shar. 'Candidate, what is your name and your rank?'

Shar swallowed, wishing her throat wasn't so dry. 'I am Shar Tillmer, Novice of the Sisterhood.'

'And what is your purpose here?'

'To pledge an oath before the gods, and to hear that oath witnessed by an initiate of the Circle.'

'Do you come of your own free will?'

'I do.'

Hestor nodded. 'Then turn now, and in proper reverence make your oath.'

Shar's heart pounded as she faced the statue once more. She spread her arms wide, bowed her head, and said, 'I swear that I will not return to the Sisterhood Cot in West High Land, but will stay at the castle of the Star Peninsula until those who plot against the High Initiate have been unmasked.' Now she raised her head and gazed steadily at the statue. 'In the name of Yandros of Chaos, and in the name of Aeoris of Order, this is my oath. And I ask that Hestor Ennas, initiate of the Circle, shall bear witness to it.'

Hestor took a pace forward. 'In the names of Aeoris and Yandros, I, Hestor Ennas, initiate of the Circle, duly bear witness to the oath pledged by Shar Tillmer.'

There was a brief silence. Then Hestor said, 'There. It's done – and no one can make you break it!'

Shar was about to reply when a sound from behind them forestalled her – rapid footsteps. Alarmed, she turned her head and saw two figures moving towards them from the direction of the door.

'What is this?' It was her uncle, his astonishment and outrage echoing through the Marble Hall as he emerged from the mist. And at his side, to Shar's horror, was the High Initiate.

'Hestor! Shar!' Neryon's voice was a furious hiss. 'What do you think you are doing? Answer me – *at once*!'

It was Shar and Hestor's sheer bad luck that the High Initiate's personal steward had not yet gone to bed and had seen them making their way towards the library. After pondering for some time whether he should interfere, the steward had at last gone in search of his master, and had found Neryon and Thel taking a late-night glass of wine together in Neryon's study.

Neryon was angry enough that Hestor had flouted the Circle's rules by entering the Marble Hall in the first place, but when the boy confessed what they had done, his anger erupted into fury.

'An Oath Ceremony?' The High Initiate's eyes blazed. 'You *dare* to use the Circle's rites on a juvenile, flippant and careless whim? This is an absolute profanity!'

'But sir,' Hestor protested desperately, 'it was the only way to—'

'It was the only way you could think of to defy my authority as Shar's legal guardian!' Thel snapped. 'Not to mention the authority of your High Initiate! Great gods, if you were my ward I'd take the skin from your back for this!'

'Oh, he'll be severely punished, Thel, be assured of it,' Neryon said darkly. 'But before I consider what steps to take, I'll make one thing clear. To both of you.' Now his glare took in Shar as well.

'The Circle's rites are solemn and serious, and I will *not* tolerate their use for trivial purposes! We arrived too late to stop the Oath Ceremony being performed. But as High Initiate, I declare it null and void.'

Shar looked horrified, and Hestor started to protest. 'Sir, you can't! Shar has made a promise to the gods, and—'

'Who do you think you are, boy, to lecture me?' Neryon interrupted ferociously. Hestor and Shar both flinched back – but suddenly Shar gave a cry and clasped both hands to the sides of her head.

'What—' The High Initiate stopped in his tracks.

'Shar? Shar, what's the matter with you?' Thel demanded anxiously.

'I—' Shar clenched her teeth, shaking her head violently. 'Ohh, it *hurts*!'

Abruptly the mists of the Marble Hall swirled and agitated, and the floor vibrated as a deep, throbbing sound began to pulsate through the air. Thel uttered a shocked oath and looked wildly round – then Shar cried out again.

And, with a whistle of air and a rush of heat and cold together, a host of elementals erupted out of nowhere into the Marble Hall.

Neryon looked stunned as a storm of tiny flames, snowflakes, feathers and leaves whirled in mad confusion around him. Gathering his wits, he opened his mouth to shout a banishing spell, but before he could utter the first words the elementals fused into a small tornado with Shar as their target. Spinning ever more turbulently, they gathered over her head. Then they spread out, forming a shape above her, and the High Initiate's eyes widened in amazement as he recognised it.

It was a seven-rayed star – the symbol of the gods of Chaos.

The star pulsed once, hugely, sending a vivid splash of light across the Hall. Then, with a *smack* of displaced air that echoed between the pillars, the elementals vanished as suddenly and explosively as they had come.

The mists were still again. The throbbing sound stopped. And with a gasp, Shar fell to the floor.

Neryon said softly, 'Great gods . . .' and Hestor ran to Shar's side, crouching down to take her by the shoulders. But she hadn't fainted; she had simply collapsed, and with his help she managed to struggle into a sitting position. Thel was staring at her, and his face was white.

'Shar,' he said at last in a stern, shaking voice, 'What do you mean by calling on those creatures?'

'She didn't call on them!' Hestor retorted fiercely. 'No one did – they came of their own accord!'

'The boy's right, Thel,' Neryon said. 'Even a high-ranking adept can't perform an elemental summoning with no preparation and no ritual. I couldn't have done it, and neither could you.'

Thel had to admit that was true. 'Then it was a trick,' he said sourly. 'Elementals are attracted to Shar, and we both know the creatures' love of mischief!'

'I don't think this was mischief,' said Neryon, and Shar saw that his expression was very serious. 'You saw the sign they formed, Thel. No elemental would dare to make mockery of Chaos's own symbol. I believe . . .' He hesitated, while his gaze fixed with unnerving steadiness on Shar's face. 'I believe that this is a sign from the gods. And I don't think it would be wise of us to ignore it.'

Thel argued, but the High Initiate was adamant. The eerie incident was, in his view, a clear omen, and until its meaning could be examined and understood, Shar must stay on at the castle. If the gods were taking an interest in her, he said, it was the Circle's duty to find out why. As a former adept himself, surely Thel must agree?

Thel had no choice but to give way, but the look he flicked at Shar and Hestor as he yielded to Neryon's wishes told them that he was very far from pleased. He left the Marble Hall a few minutes later, and when he had gone the High Initiate turned to Shar.

'You'd better go to bed,' he said, sternly but not unkindly. 'And I sincerely hope, Shar, that while you are at the castle, there won't be any more flagrant breaches of the Circle's rules!'

Shar flushed crimson, and Hestor said, 'But sir, if we hadn't broken the rules, then we'd never have known about—'

'That's enough, Hestor!' Neryon turned a raking look on him, and at the forbidding tone Hestor fell silent. 'We know nothing with any certainty. And you've caused enough trouble – any further disobedience and I'll seriously consider whether you have a future with the Circle at all! Now, escort Shar back to her room. And in the morning you'd better tell your mother that she will be staying with us.'

Hestor took Shar's arm as she was still a little unsteady on her feet and they hurried from the Marble Hall as quickly as they could. Neither of them spoke while they went through the dark library and up the stairs, but as they emerged into the fresh air of the courtyard Hestor let out his breath in a huge sigh.

Shar didn't respond. She felt shaken to the roots of her being by what had happened in the Marble Hall. Why had the elementals done what they had? She hadn't called them; hadn't even been thinking about them until the moment when they appeared. And the seven-rayed star they had formed . . . the emblem of Chaos. A sign, or so the High Initiate believed, from the gods themselves. But *why*? She was nobody, she had no powers; why in all the world should the lords of Chaos have any interest in her?

A peculiar, fearful sensation crawled along Shar's back, as if a small kitten were climbing determinedly up her spine. She looked around her at the brooding black walls and at the vastness of the sky beyond. The stars were like eyes, watching her; far below, the sea sighed and murmured like a voice whispering words which she couldn't quite hear.

And somewhere in one of the castle's guest rooms was her uncle, thwarted and angry . . .

Hestor gripped her hand suddenly and squeezed it. 'Come on.' His voice was gentle. 'We'd better go inside.'

She nodded. She didn't want to stay out here, with the eyes of the stars – and, perhaps, other eyes too – watching her. They slipped through a side door and made their way through the passages to their rooms. As they neared Shar's door, a shadow that wasn't cast by their candles moved in the corridor.

Shar gave a stifled squeak of alarm, and Hestor's hand went reflexively to his belt, though he wore no weapon. 'Who is it?' he hissed. 'Show yourself!'

The shadow moved again, and a figure emerged into the candlelight.

'Kitto!' Relief and anger coloured Hestor's voice. 'What are you doing?'

'Waiting for you.' The black-haired boy's eyes flicked eagerly from one to the other of their faces. 'What happened? Did you do the ceremony?'

Shar uttered a funny little laugh, and Hestor said, 'Oh, yes. But that was just the start of it.' He glanced over his shoulder along the passage. 'Let's all go into Shar's room, and we'll tell you.'

The two cats were waiting and curled beside Shar as she sat down on her bed with the boys flanking her. Kitto listened wide-eyed to the story, and when it was finished he whistled softly between his teeth. 'Aeoris and Yandros!' Hastily he made the splay-fingered sign to show that he meant no disrespect. 'Well, that's one in the eye for Shar's uncle!'

'It's more than that,' Hestor told him. 'If you'd seen his face when he had to give way – he was *furious*.'

Kitto frowned. 'He won't give up, of course.'

Shar tensed. 'What do you mean?'

'Well, it's obvious, isn't it? If he's really determined to take you away from the castle, and it's pretty clear that he is, then he won't let this put him off for long.'

Shar shivered. 'He can't make me go back to the Cot. Not after tonight.'

'All the same,' Hestor said, 'we have to be very careful. You should keep well out of his way until he leaves.'

Shar bit her lip. She couldn't, she wouldn't believe that Thel was an enemy. It seemed impossible. Yet tonight her fears had grown stronger.

'Yes,' she said. 'Yes, I think you're right, Hestor.' And silently in her mind she thought: *Dear gods, please, please don't let my suspicions be true!*

9

The sun had only just risen and pale daylight was trickling through the castle's windows when Thel Starnor made his way along a corridor in the east wing. Few people were up and about yet, but nonetheless, when he reached a certain door, he paused and looked back to ensure that no one was in sight. Then, satisfied, he knocked and went in.

The occupier of the room was expecting him, and as they sat down together Thel told the story of events in the Marble Hall. When he finished, the other drew in a sharp breath of disquiet.

'This adds weight to what we already know about your niece, Thel. But it is also a great setback to our plans. While the girl stays in the castle, the next stage simply can't begin.'

'I couldn't argue the point without raising awkward questions in Neryon Voss's mind,' Thel said. 'A former adept who was ready to ignore an omen like that – it would have made him very suspicious.'

'Quite. But it's vital that we have her back under our control. The question is, how to achieve it without showing our hand to Neryon.'

'I have an idea about that,' Thel said. 'It will arouse the High Initiate's suspicions, but that's a risk we must take. Besides, without solid evidence he can prove nothing, and by the time he has evidence, it will be too late.'

His companion smiled dryly. 'He'll also be too busy with preparations for the double eclipse to spare time for a thorough investigation. Very well, I agree. What is your suggestion?'

'We have to do two things,' Thel said. 'One: remove Shar from the castle, and two: ensure that she co-operates with us from now on. The first will depend on you and the men in your pay, and shouldn't be difficult if it's planned with care. And the second . . . that could prove harder, but for one thing. Shar seems to be growing fond of that wretched boy Hestor Ennas. We can use that fondness to make certain that she won't dare to disobey us again.'

Thel left the castle later that morning, Shar was surprised and very relieved, and Hestor, when he heard the news, said thankfully that they might at last be able to relax, at least for a little while.

Two days passed before they all discovered how wrong he was.

There had been a party in the castle's great hall, to celebrate the birth-anniversary of one of Hestor's friends. Such events were always open to anyone who cared to come, and so Shar and Kitto both had their first real taste of the castle's social life. When the huge spread of food had been eaten there was music and dancing; Kitto couldn't dance and so sat wistfully on the sidelines, but Shar wasn't short of partners. She danced four sets with Hestor, then stepped out with another young first-rank initiate, an older friend of Pellis's, and even the castle's senior physician. Between dances others talked to her, setting out to make her welcome, and for the first time since her arrival she began to feel almost as though she was a part of the community.

The revels were still going on when she left the hall and went to bed. She was pleasantly tired and, lulled by the purring of five cats which had all found places for themselves on her bed, she was asleep within minutes.

Three hours later, something woke her. She opened her eyes, blinking in surprise to find that the room was still dark, then sat up with a start of alarm as a peculiar little breeze wafted against her face.

Rubbing sleep from her eyes Shar told herself that it must have been the remnants of a dream; she had simply left the window open, that was all. The castle was quiet now, the party over. She should try to get back to sleep.

Suddenly from the end of her bed came a sharp hiss, and a small silhouette moved on the counterpane. At the same moment Shar felt the breeze again and then another sensation, like a prickle of heat, on her arm.

Elementals? Yes – she could see them now, several of them; creatures of air and fire darting about the room in zigzag patterns. They had startled the cats, which were all on their feet, arching their backs and growling. Whyever had they come – what did they want with her now?

'Little ones!' Shar whispered urgently. 'Little ones, what are you doing?'

The elementals began to dive and weave more agitatedly, and she sensed a psychic rush of alarm from them. They were trying to tell her something, warn her of something, but the feelings they projected were too confused to make any sense.

'Stop this!' Shar's voice grew firmer, and she raised her hands, trying to call the creatures to her and soothe them. 'Calm now; be calm. Try to tell me what – *ahh*!'

Her words broke off as the door of her room suddenly burst open. In the flaring light of a lantern Shar saw three figures coming at her; at the same instant the elementals uttered a whistling chorus of alarm – then two of the figures lunged forward. Shar tried to fling herself out of reach, but she wasn't fast enough; powerful hands clamped on her arms and she was wrenched back. The third shadowy figure moved, advancing towards her. With the strength of desperation she started to struggle, kicking and biting. The elementals shrieked again, diving, and suddenly the room was in pandemonium as they and the cats joined in the fray, the cats spitting and yowling and clawing as they tried to come to the rescue of their friend.

A flash like trapped lightning skittered across the room, and a voice – Shar had heard that voice somewhere before! – called out the words of a spell. The elementals ricocheted back; they tried to rally again to Shar's aid, but again they were driven off. And in the light of the wildly swaying lantern Shar saw the face of the man who had conjured the spell.

'*You*!' Outrage slammed into her mind, and, sensing it, two cats launched themselves at the man. One clung scrabbling and biting to his arm, the other landed on his shoulder, raking at his face with its claws; he shook them off, then snarled a harsh command.

'Hold the girl still!'

Shar saw the cloth he held in his hand and tried to twist aside but her jaw was caught in a vice-like grasp. The cloth came down, clamping over her face; she couldn't stop herself from drawing breath, and a sharp, acrid sting filled her mouth and nostrils. She tried to fight it, not to let it take hold of her, but her head was already spinning, and the room was spinning, and everything was going darker . . .

Her body sagged limply, and as her captors released their grip on her she slumped unconscious on the mattress.

Hestor was dreaming when the extraordinary noise began, and when he opened his eyes he thought at first that it was a part of the dream which he hadn't quite shaken off. But after a few seconds he realised that the sound was still continuing. A kind of wailing, which seemed to be coming from outside his window.

Still a little groggy, he stumbled out of bed and groped his way to the window in the dark. As he pulled back the curtains, he started violently – for two small faces with huge eyes were staring back at him.

The castle cats had their own network of walkways about the great building; a maze of ledges and gutters and roof-ridges which they used as easily as humans used the inner corridors. When their effort to save Shar had failed, the animals immediately went to Hestor, and now all five of them were on the ledge directly outside his room. As soon as Hestor appeared at the window, their chorus redoubled. And a faint telepathic message reached Hestor's mind. A warning of danger . . .

Hastily Hestor pulled the window open and the cats poured in like water from an overturned jug. They crowded round him, still crying, butting their hard little heads against his legs and projecting a jumble of images. Hestor wasn't especially good at communicating with cats, but what he picked up was enough to alarm him. Shar – a lantern – elementals – and fear.

Hestor grabbed a candle and ran across the room and out into the corridor. Shar's room was only a few doors away; he reached it and knocked loudly, not caring whether he woke half the castle. There was no answer, and after waiting a few seconds he pushed the door open.

The curtains were closed and the room was dark. Fumbling, Hestor lit his candle, and as the flame sprang to life he moved towards Shar's bed . . . then stopped.

The room was tidy and undisturbed. There were no signs of trouble. But the bed was neatly made and empty, with a folded nightgown lying on the pillows. Shar was not there.

Hestor raised the candle high and turned slowly round, as if expecting Shar to appear suddenly from the shadows. The cats had followed him and now started hissing. And there was a feeling in the air, one which an ordinary person would not sense but which was detectable to even the most junior Circle initiate . . . the feeling of magical energy.

One of the cats made a threatening noise in its throat. Hestor looked at it shrewdly.

'You know what's happened, don't you?' he said.

The cat growled and lashed its tail.

'Yes, I know you do. I just wish to all the gods that I could read the pictures you're sending to me more clearly.' He paused. 'All right. I'm going to wake my mother, and I want you to come with me. Can you understand? Maybe she'll be able to make more sense of what you're trying to say!'

Whether the cats comprehended or not, they all followed him as he left the room. Pellis was astonished and, at first, annoyed to be woken at such an hour, but when she heard Hestor's story her attitude changed.

The cats gathered round, miaowing, and Pellis picked up the noisiest, staring hard into its eyes. After a few moments, however, she shook her head, sighed and released the animal.

'It's no good, Hestor; I can't make any more sense of their messages than you could. But something certainly is wrong.'

'Shar's been kidnapped,' Hestor said. 'I know she has!'

'We can't be sure, but I have to admit it looks likely.' Pellis stood up and went to the window, where she pulled back the curtain. 'It's nearly dawn. I think we should make a more thorough search of Shar's room, and perhaps a few other places, and if there's still no trace of her I'll alert the High Initiate.'

Hestor watched her. 'Mother,' he said slowly, 'this proves one thing, doesn't it? Shar's uncle was here only two days ago, and now Shar has disappeared. It's too great a coincidence.'

Pellis looked over her shoulder at him. 'It doesn't prove anything, Hestor; not for certain,' she replied uneasily. 'But . . . I think you may be right.'

Within two hours, Hestor, Pellis and Kitto, who had joined the search, were certain that Shar was no longer in the castle. But they found only two clues to her disappearance: her coat and outdoor shoes were not in her room, and a pony had gone missing from the stables. On the surface, that made it look as if she had left of her own accord – but, as Hestor said, it *proved* nothing whatever. He still believed Shar had been kidnapped. And he was equally certain that Thel was behind it.

At last Pellis went to see the High Initiate. When he heard the story, Neryon's face became grave.

'Certainly it looks suspicious, and the coincidence of Thel's visit here can't be ignored,' he said. 'And if he has taken Shar back by stealth, it suggests that he wants to hide something from us. The thought of what that could be . . . it seems impossible to credit!'

'I share your feelings,' Pellis sympathised. 'Yet, as you said, the coincidence . . .'

'I know; I know.' Neryon sighed heavily. 'Well, we must make sure of our facts. Obviously my first concern is for Shar's safety. I'll organise a search party to comb the immediate area of the mountains, and I'll also send a messenger-bird to the West High Land Cot, to see if Shar has returned there.' He looked at Pellis, 'It could be that she changed her mind about wanting to stay here. Perhaps the incident in the Marble Hall frightened her and made her feel out of her depth.'

'That is a possibility,' said Pellis. The she frowned. 'But quite honestly, Neryon, knowing Shar, I doubt it very much.'

'That's the trouble,' the High Initiate replied. 'So do I.'

* * *

Shar regained consciousness to find herself being jolted along in total darkness. With a gasp she sat up, then realised that she was alone inside a small, windowless carriage which was rumbling at a tremendous pace along a rough road.

Where was she being taken? Memory of what had happened flooded back, and in rising panic Shar groped in the dark, searching for the carriage door. She had a wild idea of throwing it open and hurling herself out, but when she found the door it had been locked from the outside and would not move.

Suddenly the carriage swerved aside and began to slow down. Shar heard muffled voices; a horse whinnied, and a few minutes later they came to a halt. Footsteps sounded outside and she tensed, her heart starting to pound violently, as someone approached. There was the rattle of a bolt being drawn – then the door opened, letting in a flood of blinding daylight, and Shar looked straight into the frostily smiling face of Sister Malia.

'Well, Shar, so you have come back to us.' There was satisfaction in Malia's eyes. 'Get out, please.'

Shar's fists clenched. 'You can't do this!' she hissed. 'The High Initiate will—'

'The High Initiate doesn't concern me, or you for that matter,' Malia interrupted smoothly. 'Now, get out. You may walk or be carried, as you please, but either way you will do as you are told!'

As if to emphasise her warning, two men stepped into view and stared threateningly at Shar, and Shar's momentary hope that she might push Malia aside and make her escape died. So with as much dignity as she could muster she stepped down from the carriage.

The white buildings of the Sisterhood Cot gleamed in the bright afternoon, but the place seemed strangely deserted as Shar was led towards Sister Malia's office. Bitterly she guessed that Malia must have found some excuse for keeping the other Sisters indoors, so that her arrival wouldn't be witnessed. There was nowhere to run to, and no one she could turn to for help.

They reached the office. Malia opened the door and the two men pushed Shar inside.

And Thel rose from the chair where he had been sitting.

Shar stopped dead and stared at her uncle. Unlike Sister Malia, Thel wasn't smiling. He simply looked cold – and dangerous.

'Uncle . . .' And suddenly the fury that Shar had been bottling up burst out in a bitter flood. 'How could you do this?' she blazed at him. 'Having me kidnapped, and brought here against my will – how *could* you?'

Thel signed to Malia to close the door. His expression didn't change but he stood up and Shar backed away a pace. She had never seen him like this before. It was as if the pleasant, kindly man she had known all her life had been replaced by a complete – and sinister – stranger.

'I've no further interest in playing games with you, Shar,' he said. 'The simple fact is, you have been brought away from the castle and you will not be returning there.' Then he gave a thin smile. 'At least, not for a while yet; but that's another matter.'

Shar's head came up sharply. 'What do you mean?'

The smile still hovered. 'As yet, my dear, that's none of your concern. Suffice it to say that you have an important part to play in our plans. So important, in fact, that we must take steps to ensure you don't make any more foolhardy attempts to escape our supervision.'

In that moment, Shar knew the truth.

'You traitor! You're plotting to—' Then suddenly she stopped, horrified, as she realised what she was saying.

Thel raised his eyebrows. 'Plotting? So you've guessed a little more than we thought, have you? Mmm, yes; I suspected that your troublesome elemental friends might have told you rather more than was desirable. Well, it hardly matters, my dear. Not now that we have you safely back with us.'

'My friends at the castle won't sit by and do nothing!' Shar flared. 'When they find me gone, the High Initiate will—'

'Be too busy with more important matters to do any more than want reassurance that you're safe and well,' Thel interrupted smoothly. 'Which, of course, he shall have. And if you think that incident in the

Marble Hall will make any difference, I assure you you're wrong.'

'He said it was a sign from the gods!'

'And do you really think the gods would trouble themselves over one insignificant girl like you? No, Shar. It was a sign – certainly it was a sign. But the High Initiate doesn't know its true significance.'

Fear began to crawl through Shar's veins. 'I don't understand . . .'

'Of course you don't. But you will. When the time is right. Now,' Thel moved to Malia's desk and picked up a pen, 'we must deal with some practical matters. Firstly, you will write two letters that I will dictate to you. One will be to the High Initiate, explaining your reasons for deciding to run away back to the Cot and apologising for all the trouble you've caused. And the other will be to the boy Hestor, saying much the same but in a less formal way.'

Shar stared at him. 'I'll do no such thing! If you think you can force me—'

'Oh but I *do* think so.' Thel paused, studying her face. 'You've become close to that boy, haven't you? Indeed, you're very fond of him. As you've no doubt realised, I have a number of friends at the castle. So if you don't write the letters, I will be forced to send those friends a signal, and when they receive it, Hestor will meet with a very unpleasant, perhaps even fatal, accident.'

Shar's face turned white. 'You wouldn't . . .'

He shrugged. 'Put it to the test, if you like. It makes no difference to me.'

Shar stood rigid. She couldn't call his bluff. When she was snatched from the castle she had seen the face of one of his accomplices, and she knew that that man was in the perfect position to carry out the threat and get away with it. For Hestor's sake, she couldn't take the risk.

Her eyes filled with anguish and her shoulders drooped in defeat, and Thel knew that he had won. He smiled again, a smile that made her shiver.

'Very well. I think we understand each other.' He held out the pen, offering it to her. 'Sit down, Shar. And when we've finished the letters, we'll see about moving you to your new quarters.'

'New quarters?'

'Naturally, it won't be practical for you to stay here with the Sisters. Too many questions would be asked. So you are to have a new home, Shar.' His eyes narrowed with chilly triumph. 'A place where your real training can begin at last.'

10

The search party organised by Neryon Voss found no trace of Shar, and before noon a messenger-bird was sent winging to the West High Land Cot, asking if the Sisters there had heard any word of her. By late afternoon no reply had come.

Then, just before sunset, a dark speck came arrowing in from the mountains to hover above the castle walls. From his window Hestor saw one of the falconers emerge into the courtyard with a lure to call the bird down, and he flung himself out of his room and raced down the main staircase.

'Amit! Amit, is it a West High Land bird?'

The falconer looked at him in surprise. 'It is that – but its letter is for the High Initiate.' He paused. 'Were you expecting something?'

Belatedly Hestor remembered that, with their enemies unknown, it wasn't wise to arouse any suspicions. 'Ah . . . no, but my mother was,' he said. 'From her cousin in Wester Reach. Never mind; it'll come in a day or two I don't doubt.' Then, appearing casual, he held out a hand. 'Would you like me to take that to the High Initiate for you?'

Amit gave him a faintly suspicious look, then shrugged. 'As you please. Saves me a task. Here, then.'

Forcing himself not to run this time, Hestor went back into the castle and knocked at the door of the High Initiate's study. Neryon was there, and when the boy mutely handed over the package he opened it at once.

'Sir, is it from—?' Hestor began.

Neryon raised a hand, silencing him, as he read a sheet of paper contained in the package. Tension built suffocatingly in the room, then at last the High Initiate said, 'This is from Sister Malia. She says that Shar returned to the Cot on horseback earlier today. She has been chastised for making such a dangerous journey alone, but she's safe and well.' He looked up at Hestor, then added, 'And if you were about to suggest that Sister Malia is lying, Hestor, you'd better read this.' He held out another piece of folded paper. 'It's a letter to you, from Shar.'

Nonplussed, Hestor took the paper. It was, indeed, Shar's handwriting.

Dear Hestor,

I decided last night that I just can't stay on at the castle. It's very hard to explain, but what happened in the Marble Hall made me realise that I don't want to get any more deeply involved. I feel out of my depth, and I realise now that I'd rather be here at the Cot. I expect that makes me a coward, but I truly can't help it.

Please thank your mother for all her kindness to me, and tell her that I'm very sorry indeed to have caused her so much trouble. And I hope you, too, can find it in your heart to forgive

Your friend

Shar

'She has also sent a letter to me,' Neryon said. 'I imagine the message is much the same.' He paused. 'Is it her handwriting?'

'Yes, it is,' said Hestor. 'But I don't trust this, sir! Even if Shar is at the Cot, I don't believe she went there of her own free will!'

Neryon looked hard at him, as if debating with himself how honest it was wise to be. Then he sighed. 'In truth, Hestor, I'm inclined to agree. But short of going to the Cot and demanding her return, there's nothing I can do to dispute this. Willingly or not, Shar did write these letters, and we have no concrete evidence that she was taken away by force. Without such evidence, my hands are tied.'

Hestor silently cursed the whole rigmarole of law and protocol that had put them in this position. 'But sir, you could go to the Cot—' he began urgently.

'No, Hestor, I will not. Firstly, as I said, there's the question of evidence; and secondly I simply haven't the time to spare! And before you even think of it, I forbid you to go there.' His mouth set in a hard line. 'For one thing, and especially after your last experience, it could be an extremely dangerous venture.'

Hestor realised then what the High Initiate was tacitly saying to him. Neryon, too, was now becoming convinced that something was afoot and that Thel Starnor and Sister Malia were involved in it. He looked searchingly back at Neryon, and the High Initiate gave him a small, wintry smile.

'I think it's better if we don't discuss this any further at the moment, Hestor,' he said. 'But I don't intend to abandon my own investigations. And if you and the boy Kitto unearth anything that might be useful, I want to hear of it.'

It was unspoken permission to make their own explorations, and relief flooded through Hestor like a tide. 'I understand, sir,' he said. He turned to go, then paused at the door and looked back. 'Thank you.'

Hestor was in the corridor leading to his apartments when someone shouted his name and he looked round to see Kitto racing towards him.

'Hestor!' The black-haired boy was breathless with excitement. 'Hestor, I've discovered something! Quick, let's go into your room!' He grabbed Hestor's arm, propelling him into a run.

'It can't be anything to what's happened to me!' Hestor tried to shake Kitto off and wave Shar's letter under his nose at the same time, but Kitto took no notice, and as they entered the room they were both trying to shout each other down. Hestor won the tussle, and at last Kitto subsided enough to listen to his story of the messenger-bird's arrival and the news it had brought. When Hestor finished, Kitto's blue eyes blazed with anger.

'Can't stay on at the castle – I don't believe it!' he said ferociously.

'I know. But the High Initiate says that without evidence that she was kidnapped, there's nothing he can do.'

Kitto uttered a sharp laugh. 'Well, we've got evidence now!'

Hestor tensed. 'What do you mean?'

'I've just been to see the physician, Lemor something . . .'

'Lemor Carrick.'

'That's him. And Physician Lemor Carrick has got scratches all over his face and arms. *Cat* scratches.'

Hestor stared at him. '*What*?'

'Yes, and they look pretty new. So how did he get them?'

'Great gods . . . the cats that came and woke me last night! They must have tried to protect Shar!'

'Right. And Physician Carrick knows all about drugs, doesn't he?'

'So he'd have known what to use to make Shar unconscious.' And Carrick was also a fifth rank adept, Hestor reminded himself. Which could explain the echoes of magical energy he had felt in Shar's room . . .

'Carrick's one of them' said Kitto. 'Question is,

what are we going to do about it?' He paused. 'Do we tell the High Initiate?'

'No. No, not yet.' Hestor frowned, thinking hard. One thing in particular had baffled him since the beginning of this affair and that was the reason why Thel wanted to keep Shar away from the castle. There were, he thought, two possibilities: either there was something here that he didn't want Shar to discover, or he had another use for her – which was possibly connected with the assassination plot. Whichever was true, it seemed to suggest that Shar was special in some way.

And what had happened in the Marble Hall added to the fire. 'Come on.' He jumped suddenly to his feet, startling Kitto. 'There's something I want to do.'

'What?'

'Go to the library, and start searching.' For the likeliest place to find answers was surely among the castle records. Shar had been born here, after all, and her parents both died here. If there truly was something special about her, something that Thel was trying to conceal, the library was where the clue would be found.

'Searching?' Kitto asked. 'Whatever for?'

'I'll explain on the way.' Hestor was at the door, impatience mounting as his idea took hold. 'Come *on*!'

Kitto shrugged and followed him out of the room.

A lot of the castle-dwellers were taking their evening

meal at this hour, so the boys had the library to themselves. Kitto couldn't read but he fetched and carried books as Hestor searched for the records relating to the deaths of Shar's parents.

It wasn't long before he found what he wanted – and with it a further mystery.

Thel's version of the story was perfectly true. Shar's father had died in the Marble Hall, caught by a backlash of occult energy when a ritual being performed by several high-ranking adepts went wrong. There was nothing suspicious about that; such tragedies happened occasionally. But the record made no mention of the ritual's nature or of precisely what had happened, and that puzzled Hestor.

'These details should always be written down,' he told Kitto. 'It's a basic safeguard, to make sure that the same mistakes aren't made again. But there's no entry about it at all.'

Kitto stared at the page, though the writing meant nothing to him. 'What about Shar's mother?' he asked. 'Is there anything about her?'

'I'll look.' Hestor flipped pages. 'Ah . . . yes, here. It says . . .'

His voice tailed off and Kitto said, 'What? What does it say? She jumped into the sea, didn't she?'

Hestor touched his tongue to his lower lip. 'That's what Shar's always been told. But this is just a bit different. According to this entry, it was presumed she jumped off the stack, but no one knows for certain. Because her body was never found.'

Kitto whistled softly. 'That opens up a whole new sack of trinkets!'

'Quite. If they didn't find her, then it's possible she didn't kill herself at all.'

The boys looked at each other for several seconds, both thinking the same thing but neither wanting to be first to voice it. It was a wild surmise, but Shar's mother could have been murdered. And if she was, then the death of Shar's father also began to look very suspicious.

'Wait,' Hestor said suddenly. 'There's something I want to check.'

He turned back to the record of Shar's father's death and studied the page again. Then he found it . . .

He had overlooked it before, but the record listed the adepts who had taken part in the fateful ritual. There were seven names in all – and two of them stood out like fire in darkness.

Thel Starnor and Lemor Carrick.

This was too great a coincidence to be ignored, and Kitto wondered immediately if the other names on the list might give a clue to any other possible traitors in the Circle. But when Hestor checked the records of adepts, he made another discovery. Apart from Thel and Lemor, every other person who had witnessed the ritual had died in the past few years.

'They were all quite old,' he said when he finally closed the book. 'But all the same . . .'

Kitto nodded. Even if the adepts were old, it would have been easy enough for a physician to help them out of the world before their time, with no one any the wiser.

The next clue Hestor wanted to search for concerned Shar herself, and he fetched a volume of birth records. Before long he had found Shar's entry, and he began to comb it for a hint of anything out of the ordinary.

'Well, she was born at night, so her birth-celebration would have been dedicated to Chaos rather than Order,' he said.

Kitto, who had no idea when or where he had been born, and doubted whether he had had a birth-celebration at all, shrugged. 'So? Everybody's supposed to be dedicated to one or the other.'

'I was thinking about what happened in the Marble Hall. The seven-rayed star . . . that fits in. Oh, and it says there was a Warp storm going on at the time—'

'Ha!' said Kitto sharply. 'Of course – it makes sense! She's a Daughter of Storms.'

Hestor was completely baffled. 'She's a what?'

'A Daughter of Storms.' The black-haired boy stared back. 'Do you mean you don't know what that is?'

'No,' said Hestor.

Astonished, Kitto told him. Where he came from, he said, it was a common belief that children born during a Warp had a special kind of power. The brigands who had brought him up called them Sons and Daughters of Storms, and they had been terrified of them for it was said they could summon a Warp at will and use it to transport themselves to any location in the world.

'Remember what happened in the mountains?' Kitto finished. 'When the band attacked you?'

Hestor certainly did. If Shar did have special powers – and, from what he had already seen, Hestor was convinced of it – then this was the clue to their origin. A Daughter of Storms . . . somewhere in the archives there must be details of what that truly meant. And his mother would surely know where to look.

Kitto tensed suddenly and turned his head towards the door. 'Footsteps,' he hissed. 'Someone's coming.'

Hestor's mind snapped back to the present and he snatched up an armful of books. 'Help me put these away!' Anyone could be approaching; even Lemor Carrick. 'And get a study-book from that shelf there; in the middle, any of them will do – yes, that one!'

Two third-rank adepts entered the library moments later to find Hestor apparently teaching Kitto to read. The adepts smiled approvingly but otherwise ignored them, and the boys ended their 'lesson' and left the library a few minutes later.

Out on the stairs Hestor sighed. 'We'd probably have been quite safe carrying on with the search.'

'Or maybe we wouldn't,' Kitto replied darkly. 'When in doubt, don't trust anyone.'

'I know. You're right.' Hestor glanced back

towards the library in frustration. 'Come on. Even if we can't do any more tonight, we can at least find Mother and tell her.'

They continued up the stairs in silence.

11

Shortly after midnight, when the Sisters were soundly asleep, Thel and Sister Malia took Shar away from the Cot.

This time it was a short journey, on horseback and with the same two men guarding her to ensure she caused no trouble. Shar was too afraid for Hestor's safety to be defiant; she simply sat mute, staring around her as they followed a winding track deep into the mountains.

Before long they reached a small valley surrounded by high peaks. In the valley stood a solitary building; one of the old retreat-houses sometimes used by Senior Sisters for solitary contemplation. This one, however, had obviously been disused for a long time. It was the perfect hideaway, Shar reflected bitterly. No one would ever think to look for her here.

She was taken inside and to an upstairs room. Everything had been prepared for her, and she realised that her uncle and Sister Malia must have been planning this move for a long time. There were bars on the window and locks on the door, and any thoughts of escape were futile. She was a prisoner. And she didn't even know why.

Sister Malia brought her a plate of food, which she didn't want, and then she was locked in the room and left alone. She heard Malia's footsteps going down the stairs, then a few moments later the sound of voices drifted up from the room below. Shar was suddenly alert as she realised that Malia and her uncle were talking and she could almost make out what was being said. If she could just amplify the sound . . .

A water jug and glass stood on a table near the narrow bed. Shar snatched up the glass, upturned it on the floor, then crouched down and put her ear to it. She and other children at the High Margrave's palace had often eavesdropped on their elders this way. Now, for the first time, the game had a serious purpose.

The two voices below swam into focus. And what Shar heard sent an ice-cold sensation crawling up her spine.

'. . . to settle tonight, and then I think she'll be ready,' Sister Malia was saying. She paused. 'It won't be easy, Thel. To use someone so inexperienced on the sixth plane carries a high risk – not least to you.'

'I'm confident that I can protect myself,' Thel replied. 'And don't forget, my dear Malia, Shar is no ordinary novice. She's a Dark-Caller.'

Shar's skin prickled. A Dark-Caller? She had never heard such a phrase before.

Malia said, 'Mmm . . .' Shar could picture her face as she made the sound; her mouth pursing, her pale blue eyes taking on a hard look. She had seen that look many times. 'It all fits together very well, doesn't it?' the Sister continued. 'Shar, born during a double eclipse and now becoming the instrument of our plans at the time of a second such eclipse. Appropriate, and satisfying.' Another pause. 'More wine?'

'Thank you.' There was silence for a few moments, then Thel spoke again. 'It's extremely rare for two double eclipses to occur within such a short space of time. In fact I don't think there's a record of it ever happening before. It's a little like a gift from the gods – though under the circumstances the gods will have nothing to do with it! Yes; a very happy coincidence.'

Malia laughed, not pleasantly. 'Happy for us, if not for Neryon Voss.'

'Indeed. A toast, then. To our success – and to Shar, who will bring it about!'

Glass clinked, and then there was silence. Slowly, Shar sat back on her heels, staring blindly at the wall. She felt sick. She knew the truth now. There could be no possible doubt. Thel was not merely involved in the assassination plot; he was the leader. And he meant to use Shar as a weapon in his scheme – for she was a Dark-Caller.

Shar shivered as that name ran through her mind again and again. What did it mean? From what Thel had said, it seemed Dark-Callers had some particular power connected with the sixth plane. She knew that there were seven planes in all, the four lowest of which were the realms of Earth, Water, Fire and Air. These were the worlds of her elemental friends, and they held no terrors for her. But the three higher planes were another matter, for they were inhabited by far more powerful and dangerous entities which only a high-ranking sorcerer's skill could control. Shar was no sorcerer. So what was the Dark-Caller's power, locked within her soul, that could link her to those monstrous worlds?

Shar didn't sleep that night. As the two moons tracked slowly across the sky she paced her room like a caged animal, while anger and fear and a desperate need to do something churned her mind. But no answers came to her, and the silent, fervent prayers she sent to the gods went unanswered. She was trapped. And if she did not do what her uncle wanted of her, Hestor would die.

At last the first glimmer of dawn began to show on the high slopes of the mountains. As daylight crept into her room Shar returned to the window, staring miserably out across the overgrown remains of the retreat-house's garden. And in the undergrowth she saw something move.

It was just a small disturbance among the vegetation, but Shar's intuition was suddenly alert. And a moment later she felt a tingle in the back of her mind; a curious and cautious sense of probing.

Shar gripped the window bars and leaned forward, peering down at the ground. And a small face surrounded by ginger fur stared eagerly back at her.

'Amber!' Her eyes widened in incredulous delight as she saw the cat she had befriended. He must have sensed her presence when she arrived at the Cot, and when she was brought here, he had followed!

The cat's mouth opened in a miaow, though no sound reached her, and urgently she tried to make mental contact. Her mind projected images: herself unable to leave the room, Amber coming to her, and – most important of all – a sense of danger and secrecy. Amber continued to stare at her, still curious, but she received no answering message from his mind. Then abruptly he blinked, turned, and melted silently away into the undergrowth.

Shar stepped back from the window, her heart thumping. Had the cat understood? She had no means of knowing. All she could do was hope that somehow he would find a way to reach her. For if he did, there was a slender chance that she might use him to get a warning to the castle . . .

The daylight grew and before long she heard the sounds of other people moving about in the house, and then footsteps on the stairs announced the arrival of Sister Malia with a breakfast tray. This time Shar forced herself to eat, knowing that she might need her strength. Then, an hour later, her uncle came to see her.

Thel looked with satisfaction at the empty plate and said, 'I'm glad to see you've decided to be sensible, Shar. I trust this attitude will continue.'

Shar glared resentfully at him but didn't answer, and he went on, 'Well, time will tell . . . and you know what will happen if you give us any trouble. Now; make yourself presentable and come with me. It's time for your lessons to begin.'

'Lessons?' Shar's head came up sharply, and he smiled a thin smile.

'Oh, I don't mean schooling. This is something quite different. In fact, you might say it was what you were born to do. You see, Shar, you are an unusual girl. You always have been. Only no one else has ever taken the trouble to find out precisely what your special talent is, or how it can be used.'

Shar said angrily, 'You have no right to use me for anything! You don't own me!'

'Until you come of age, my dear, in one sense I *do* own you.' His smiled grew less pleasant. 'For your friend Hestor's sake I'd advise you to bear that in mind when we start our work. Come along; I don't want to delay any longer.'

She rose slowly to her feet and followed him from the room and down the stairs. From a table in the hallway Thel picked up a lit lamp, then they walked along a passage that led to the back of the house. At the end of the passage was a door, and as they neared it Shar began to feel uneasy. There was an unpleasant atmosphere here; not exactly a smell, more a sense of something foul and decaying. The small hairs at the back of her neck were rising, prickling, and as Thel reached to the bolt she had to crush down a sudden urge to turn and run, back along the passage, upstairs, outside, anywhere that would get her away from whatever lay behind the door.

She made an ugly choking sound, and Thel turned and looked at her. 'Don't be afraid,' he said. 'There's nothing here that can harm you. Not at present.'

Shar was beginning to feel very sick, but she forced herself to watch as he slid the bolt back and opened the door. Beyond was a flight of stone stairs, leading down into the cellars of the house. They looked dark and dank. And the feeling of evil – for that, she realised in horror, was what she had sensed – flowed up from the stairwell like a cold, clammy shroud waiting to wrap and smother her.

'No . . .' she whispered. 'Oh, no . . . please . . . I don't want to go down there!'

Thel raised the lamp, making shadows dance on the walls. He said softly, 'You know the price of disobedience, Shar.'

Hestor's face formed in her inner vision. She looked at Thel once, with loathing, then drew a deep breath and stepped forward.

The flight of stairs was short, and ended at another door, locked with a key this time. Thel opened it

. . . and Shar stood staring at the room that was revealed.

It was small, windowless and contained only a cupboard, a chair, and a table on which stood something covered by a black cloth. And it stank of sorcery. Not the sharp, exhilarating sorcery that she had tasted in the air of the castle, but a dark and ominous feeling that filled her with dread.

'This,' Thel said, 'is where your lessons will take place. And you will learn a very great deal, Shar. More than the Circle could teach you. More than you have ever dreamed possible.'

Fearfully, Shar looked up at him. 'This is something evil . . .'

'Evil?' He smiled. 'Oh, no. Not evil, my dear child, merely very, very powerful.' He closed the door, locked it, then crossed the room and set the lamp on the table. 'Tell me; do you know what a sixth-plane entity is?'

Something inside Shar seemed to freeze. She didn't answer, and after a moment her uncle shrugged. 'Well, if you either can't or won't say, it doesn't matter, for I will show you.' Abruptly his voice hardened. 'Sit down.'

Shar obeyed and sank on to the chair, which had been set facing the table. She was shaking now, and she watched as Thel went to the cupboard and took several items from it. A copper dish, a block of incense and a taper were all set on the table. Then Thel took out a piece of cord made from seven different coloured threads and with seven knots tied along its length.

'Hold the cord, and don't let go of it,' he said. 'It will protect you.'

'Protect me?' Shar echoed fearfully.

'From the power of what I will show you. You are about to look into a world you have never seen before, and that world can be hazardous. But if you do everything I tell you, instantly and without question, you'll come to no harm.'

She had no choice. She took the cord, which felt greasy and unpleasant, then tried to calm her racing pulse as Thel moved to stand behind the table. For a minute he stood still, head bowed, concentrating, and Shar felt magical energy begin to build up in the room. Only the highest Circle adepts, she knew, could summon power as easily and quickly as this, and she quailed inwardly as she realised just how great Thel's skill must be. He had been among the Circle's best – and he had forgotten nothing of his training.

Thel exhaled, and the sound echoed eerily, as if other, invisible presences were answering him. He placed the incense block in the copper dish, then touched the lit taper to it. Smoke began to curl sluggishly upwards, and almost at once Shar's nostrils caught the pungent scent.

'The incense will help attune you to the astral planes,' Thel told her softly. 'Don't fight its influence. Open your mind.'

Despite her fear of him, Shar tried to fight. She didn't want to succumb to this. Whatever it was that he intended her to see, she wanted no part of it. But the smoke was growing thicker, and the smell stronger, and there was a strange, throbbing sensation in her head that made her feel dizzy and unreal. Through a haze she saw Thel smile with grim satisfaction. Then he reached out to the shrouded object on the table and removed the black cloth.

Underneath was an oval mirror, made from darkened glass and set in a frame decorated with elemental sigils. Dim shapes shifted in its depths; for a moment Shar glimpsed her own reflection but then it changed, becoming ambiguous and menacing. She wanted to look away from it but found she couldn't; the incense had a hold of her and she could only stare, unblinking, at the phantasms in the glass.

Thel doused the lamp and the room sank into darkness. A silhouette now, he raised his hands and held them above the mirror. Shar's vision swam; at Thel's fingertips a strange light glimmered, then a hot, deep glow appeared in the glass.

'Look, Shar,' Thel said in a low, ominous voice. 'Look into the realm of earth.'

The glow strengthened and a picture took form. Shar saw rocks shot through with veins of dark colours that ran like blood, and an awful sense of heaviness and oppression seemed to crush in on her mind, as though she were being buried under thousands of tons of stone. She gasped, and through her shock heard Thel speak again.

'Hold the cord. Don't be afraid. You are moving through the planes. Look now into the world of water.'

Coldness hit her like the slap of a wave, and suddenly the mirror and her mind were heaving with images of water. A raging sea, a rushing river, rain pounding down from a thunderous sky—

'Move on. Move on. Look into the world of air.'

Now there were tumbling clouds in the mirror, and the feeling of a huge, buffeting gale rushing into the room. Shar swayed on the chair, and Thel said, 'Be calm. Look now into the world of fire.'

This time she cried out aloud, for the heat that assailed her was like being burned. In the mirror flames leaped and roared, hurling light out into the room. Thel, vividly lit by the glare, was like a figure out of a nightmare as he called above the crackling din in Shar's mind:

'*Be calm*! Hold the cord. Look now into the fifth plane . . .'

The blaze in the mirror died abruptly and the room sank into blackness. Then, deep within the glass, something stirred. Coils of silvery mist began to swirl across the mirror's surface, and bizarre faces formed in the mist. Some smiled at Shar, some scowled, some leered or threatened. And there were sounds in her mind; sighs, whispers and, once, the soft giggling of something not quite human.

Shar's heart was beating rapidly and painfully. She was afraid – she knew she was afraid – but she was also in the grip of a terrible, irresistible fascination. She was vaguely aware of Thel's shadowy figure moving behind the mirror, then he drew his hands away from it and took a step back.

'Now, Shar.' There was a quiver of excitement in his voice – excitement and, she realised, a fear that matched her own. 'Look once more. Hold the cord tightly, for you are about to be shown a realm that few adepts have ever set eyes on. Look into the world of the sixth plane . . .'

A sharp, savage pain stabbed through Shar's head, as though someone had plunged a knife into her skull. She screamed, a shrill, high-pitched note, and for the last time the mirror changed.

A sense of huge power swirled at Shar, and with it came a stench so abominable that she clapped her hands to her mouth and nose. Thel shouted, 'The cord! Hold the cord!' and with a frantic reflex her fingers closed on the thread before it could fall. Eyes wide above her cupped hands, Shar stared mesmerised at what the glass was revealing.

It – or they, for the shape forming in the mirror was so alien that it almost defied any rational sense – moved under the glass's surface with a hideous, sluggish motion, like thickly polluted water. It was so grotesque and misshapen that merely to look at it made her feel sick . . . but she could feel a dreadful intelligence emanating from it; a sense of cunning, of malignancy . . . and of dark, ravening greed. This monstrosity wanted to *devour.* And Shar knew with an appalling instinct that if it could only break through the prison of the magical mirror and into the mortal world, then even Thel's sorcery would not be enough to defy its power. It would kill. It would destroy. It would *feed* – and only when its loathsome hunger was sated would it return to its own dimension.

Horror and revulsion filled Shar's mind, but still she couldn't tear her gaze away. The incense, Thel's magic, the paralysing horror of the entity itself; all were combining to hold her rigid and helpless.

Then, slowly, the thing in the mirror began to turn. It had a head of sorts; Shar glimpsed a membranous ear, a drooling mouth, a nose like the beak of a mutated eagle. And it had eyes. Hollow sockets in the mockery of a face, they burned with a cold, colourless light like the last embers of a dead star. Those eyes swivelled. They focused on her . . . and two glaring crimson pinpoints appeared in their depths as from deep within the mirror, yet also ringing and echoing in her head, Shar heard the sound of raucous, insane laughter.

A giant hand semed to clutch at her stomach. As though from a vast distance she heard her own voice crying 'NO!', and with a violent movement she flung her hands up, gripping the cord and jerking it taut as though it could be a barrier between herself and the horror glaring at her out of the mirror. The glass flared with white light; there was a *crack*, like a window shattering—

And Shar found herself sprawling on the cellar floor, in utter darkness and utter silence.

She dragged air into her lungs. It made an awful noise and she coughed, a racking cough that hurt her ribs. She was numb with shock, and for several terrible moments she thought that she must have lost her mind; that what she had seen had turned her insane. But no; for she could make out dim shapes now, and they made sense. The chair. The table, with the now darkened and empty mirror standing upon it. And she could hear the sound of Thel breathing . . .

There came a scratch of flint and metal, and the lamp flared into life. Shar didn't move. She sensed Thel's approach, then he came to stand before her and she knew he was looking down at her.

'Well, Shar.' He spoke gently, almost kindly. It disgusted her. 'You have seen, now, the nature of the creatures that inhabit the sixth plane. Yes, you were frightened. But there is no need for you to fear them. For that, my dear, is the nature of your special talent.'

Shuddering, Shar at last looked up. 'I don't understand . . .' Her voice sounded like someone else's.

'No. But you will, soon. When I have trained you. For, thanks to a simple accident of birth, you have the power to face the creatures of the sixth plane and to command and control them. It is a rare and precious gift. And I will teach you to use it. For a purpose.' He smiled, the chilly smile of a predator. 'A very, very special purpose, for which I have been waiting since the night you were born.'

12

Shar lay shuddering on the bed in her locked room. She was wrapped in a heavy blanket but it couldn't warm her. Nothing could warm her, for the cold was in her bones, in her marrow, and it was the cold of terror and despair.

She barely remembered being brought back here. All she could think of was the quaking, blinding horror of what had happened in the cellar. And two memories in particular were burning in her mind, forcing her to relive them over and over again. The eyes and the laughter of that malignant *thing* from the sixth plane as it gazed at her out of the mirror. And Thel's voice, calmly and cruelly revealing the monstrous nature of his plans for her.

A new fit of shivering assailed her. She couldn't believe that this was truly happening – surely, *surely* it must be a nightmare and she would wake soon and find that all was well. But deep down she knew that wouldn't happen. Like a fly in a spider's web she was caught in the trap that Thel had devised for her – a trap he had been waiting to spring from the day she was born. And now she was to be his pawn, the medium through which he would summon the powers of the sixth plane in his bid to murder Neryon Voss.

Shar hadn't meant to reveal how much she knew about Thel's scheming, but fear, revulsion and bitter fury had got the better of her, and as they faced each other in the gloom of the cellar she had hurled the accusation in his face. Traitor, murderer, assassin – the words had come tumbling uncontrollably from her lips as she floundered in the aftershock of her glimpse of the sixth plane. She knew the truth, she screamed at him, and she had enough evidence to see him damned! Thel's eyes had flared with fury – for a terrible moment she had thought he would strike her – but abruptly his ferocity faded and he laughed a small, soft laugh.

'I congratulate you, Shar,' he had said mockingly. 'You are more resourceful than I'd thought, though no doubt your precious friend Hestor has given you a great deal of help. Oh, don't look so worried, my dear; Hestor is perfectly safe so long as you continue to do as you're told. So; you believe I mean to kill Neryon Voss, do you? Well, I see no reason to deny it. That is what I intend, and you, with your special abilities, are going to be the weapon in my hands.'

Something inside Shar had come close to snapping then. 'You can't use me . . . not like that . . . Those – those things of the sixth plane . . . I can't control them!'

She remembered how Thel had smiled then. 'Oh

but you can, Shar,' he said softly. 'And you will. Through you, I will summon one of those entities to the mortal world, and you will give it the command to destroy Neryon Voss.'

'No . . . I won't do it! I won't be a part of it!' Her voice had risen to a shrill pitch.

'You will,' Thel had repeated composedly. 'You see, it's too late to retreat now. For when through my sorcery you glimpsed the entities of the sixth plane, they also saw you, and recognised you as a Dark-Caller. They know you have the power to control them, and they hate you for it. The link has been forged between you and them, and so when I open the way for them to enter the mortal world, you will have a simple choice. Either you perform the ritual I shall teach you – the ritual that will ensure the High Initiate's death – or the creatures of the sixth plane will turn on you, and you will become their victim instead.' He had paused, and in the claustrophobic silence Shar heard her own pulse like a rushing river in her ears. Then Thel added, very softly, 'For all your high ideals, I don't think you have the courage to face that.'

And in the core of her heart Shar had known he was right.

She rolled over on the bed, hugging the blanket more tightly round herself and trying to blot out the anguish she felt.

Then suddenly, from behind her, she heard a noise.

With a violent jolt she sat up and turned, wide-eyed, to stare at the wall. Something was there, behind the stonework above the room's empty fireplace. It was moving with a stealthy, muffled sound, and instantly Shar's thoughts flashed back to the cellar, and the horror in the glass. Great gods, if it hadn't been fully banished; if some power from that terrible dimension had broken through – she felt panic start to rise inside her, felt her stomach and lungs and throat tightening . . .

The muffled noise came again and a cascade of soot thumped down the chimney, sending a small, black cloud billowing into the room. Shar shrank back, pushing clenched fists against her mouth. She was going to scream, she knew she was, and she wouldn't be able to stop it—

More soot fell, and this time something else came down with it. A dark shape, small, twisting in mid-air as it dropped into the hearth. And Amber, his ginger fur grimy with smuts, shook himself, stared at Shar with huge green eyes and gave a loud, complaining miaow.

'Ohhh . . .' Shar's panic collapsed into a confusion of relief and gratitude. She had completely forgotten her desperate appeal to the cat, but Amber, it seemed, had not. He had understood her message. And he had found a way to come to her.

She threw off the blanket and reached out to hug the little animal. Amber didn't purr but gazed keenly into her eyes, and she felt the anxious questioning of his thoughts.

'Oh, Amber!' Her breath was catching in her

throat; she was almost in tears and didn't know why. 'Amber, you're my only hope! You must go to the castle!' In her mind she made a picture of the road through the mountains, leading northwards to the Star Peninsula and the sea. Then an image of the castle on its stack, the great black walls, the four spires, and lastly the face of Hestor.

Amber's tail twitched and a string of muddled impressions came back to her. 'No, Amber, *no*!' Shar whispered desperately.'Try to understand, please try!' Oh, why couldn't she communicate more clearly? Her mind was so disjointed; unless she could gather her wits he would never grasp what she was trying to tell him!

She took a very deep breath. A simple message, that was the best she could hope to do. Go to the castle. Find Hestor. And tell him just three things. *Danger, the sixth plane* and *Dark-Caller*. She could ask no more of the cat, and she must pray fervently that Hestor would be able to make sense of it.

It took a long time to impress her message on Amber's mind, and she was further hampered by the fear that at any moment her uncle or Sister Malia might come upstairs and discover them. But at last Amber seemed to understand. She felt a wave of fierce affection from his mind; he rubbed his head once, hard, against her fingers, then wriggled out of her grasp and ran to the hearth. One glance back, then with a springing and scrabbling he was gone up the chimney again. Shar held her breath as she listened to him climbing, then the sounds stopped and she knew he had reached the roof. Would he know how to get to the castle? Would he be able to reach it safely? And, more vitally, would he remember his mission for long enough? There were so many uncertainties that Shar quailed inwardly. But despite her fears the spark of hope still burned. There was a chance. And, if the gods were with her, it would work.

She was shivering again now, and suddenly dreadfully tired. There was soot on the floor, and she herself was filthy with it, but she didn't care. Whatever Thel or Malia thought about the mess, they wouldn't suspect the truth. She wanted to sleep. She *needed* to sleep. And she would go to sleep with a prayer to Yandros on her lips.

With the double eclipse now only eleven days away, the High Initiate and other senior Circle adepts had begun to prepare in earnest. Neryon himself was spending a lot a time in prayer and meditation, for the responsibility he would carry on the night of the ritual was enormous. He would, effectively, stand in for the gods while 'their eyes were blinded', and his power would be the only barrier between the mortal world and the dark forces that might otherwise threaten humankind. The ritual he must perform was long and taxing; it needed many hours of study so Neryon had cut himself off from everyday castle affairs. Until his preparations were complete, anyone who wanted to see him about anything but the most urgent matters would simply have to wait.

For Hestor and Kitto, this was cause for dismay. They had told Pellis about their discoveries in the library, but though she agreed cautiously with their theory about Thel and his motives, she had refused to speak to Neryon on their behalf. This, she said, did not count as a most urgent matter, and it could keep until after the eclipse was over. And as she herself also had to prepare for the event, she couldn't spare time to help them with any more investigations.

Frustrated, but aware that Pellis couldn't be persuaded, the boys continued to search through the library archives. But they found nothing of any more real use. There were some documents concerning Sons and Daughters of Storms, but they only gave details of the Warp legend without even commenting on whether or not that legend was likely to be true.

On the fourth day they sat in the dining-hall for their evening meal and talked gloomily about their lack of progress. Not for the first time, Kitto declared that they should throw caution to the winds, defy the adults and go to the West High Land Cot to see Shar for themselves. Hestor, though, said no. Even if they could reach Shar at all, they wouldn't have a chance to talk to her privately with Sister Malia watching like a hawk; and the trouble they'd get into for disobeying the High Initiate's orders would wreck everything.

They fell silent after that, both toying morosely

with their food. Then, as he reached out to pick up his mug of beer, Kitto suddenly jumped.

'What the—' He leaned back on the bench and looked down at his feet. 'There's a cat under this table!'

'Ignore it,' Hestor said sourly. 'They're always coming in at meal times, trying to scrounge food.'

Kitto, though, was still staring at the cat. 'I can feel something,' he said in surprise. 'Like someone else's thoughts in my head. As if it's trying to talk to me.'

Hestor wasn't really interested but made an effort. 'Can you communicate with them?' he asked.

'Don't know; I've never tried. But this is weird. It's . . .' His voice tailed off, and suddenly Hestor felt a prickling of intuition as he saw the other boy's expression change.

'What's wrong?' His voice was sharp.

Kitto looked up at him. 'It just showed me a picture. Of Shar.'

As though to emphasise his words, the cat gave an urgent miaow and butted its head against Hestor's legs. Quickly Hestor ducked under the table to look at the animal.

'It's a ginger,' he said. 'And I've never seen a ginger with markings like that at the castle.'

'It's from the Cot!' Kitto hissed. 'It must be!'

Hestor sat up again. 'Shar must have sent it.' He glanced rapidly round the hall to check that no one was watching them, then leaned forward. 'Did you pick up anything else?'

Kitto shook his head. 'No. But I got a feeling of trouble.'

'So did I. Look, if the cat's brought a message from Shar we need to get it away quickly, before someone else in the hall senses anything from its mind. We'll go to my room and I'll try to make the cat understand that we want it to follow us.'

Kitto nodded and, appearing casual, they both stood up. Immediately the cat gave a protesting cry and jumped on to the bench, its tail lashing. Hestor said 'Hush!' under his breath, and reinforced it with a mental warning. Then, as best he could, he projected an image of himself and Kitto leaving the hall, and the need not to draw attention to themselves. The cat paused, looking at him – then it sat down and began to wash itself.

Amber seemed to ignore Kitto and Hestor when they walked away, but as he continued to lick his fur his green eyes were alert and surreptitiously watching. He had seen the black-haired human slip several pieces of meat into his pocket before he left, and had picked up from his mind a promise of food if he should follow them. Amber was ravenously hungry. He waited for perhaps a minute. Then he jumped down from the bench and trotted purposefully between the rows of tables towards the doors.

'It's no use.' Hestor sat back and pushed his fingers through his hair in weary frustration. 'I just can't make sense of what he's trying to tell us!'

Kitto turned round from the window seat and looked at Amber. For two hours now Hestor had been trying to untangle the string of images and thoughts that the cat projected to him, but the pictures were so hazy, and the contact so faint, that his efforts had achieved almost nothing. They knew only that the animal had been sent by Shar, and that she was being held at the Cot against her will.

Pellis was at a meeting of the Circle council so they hadn't been able to turn to her for help. Not that she could have achieved much, Hestor reflected unhappily, for she, like himself, didn't have the true knack of communicating with cats. The High Initiate would have been another matter, but he too was at the council meeting and even when he emerged the boys wouldn't be allowed to approach him.

Kitto slid off the seat and came to crouch beside the bed. He stroked Amber's head, producing a purr. 'All right,' he said. 'What have you got from him so far?'

'Only what I've told you. Shar's in trouble, Thel Starnor's responsible, and there's danger. And I keep getting something about the number six, but I've no idea what that signifies.'

Kitto shrugged, for numbers meant no more to him than letters. 'If it's a clue, it beats me. Six. It's—' He stopped.

Amber's ears had pricked suddenly, and the cat was staring intently at him. Kitto blinked, then looked at Hestor in astonishment.

'Planes!' he said.

'What?'

'Planes! I heard it in my head, clear as anything!' He pointed at the cat. 'When I said "six" he sent the word to me!'

Hestor crouched forward, staring first at Amber and then at Kitto. 'Maybe you've got the talent – you said you've never tried, but maybe you've got it! Kitto, try again! See if you can pick up anything more!'

Eagerly Kitto concentrated, his face creasing into a frown. He gazed at the cat, and Amber looked back at him with sudden interest.

'Six . . .' Kitto said again after a few moments, then, 'No – not six, sixth. Sixth . . . plane.' His frown deepened. 'That doesn't make any sense.'

Hestor, however, had tensed, and colour drained from his face. 'Oh yes it does,' he whispered. 'Kitto, this is vital! What else is he saying?'

Kitto redoubled his efforts, shutting his eyes now as he strove to understand Amber's message. A minute passed, then two, then three. At last the black-haired boy shook his head and exhaled, like a swimmer coming up for air. He opened his eyes and looked at Hestor.

'Two things,' he said. 'That's all.'

'What are they? Tell me!'

'The double eclipse – that's important in some way, but I don't think the cat knows any more. And the words "Dark-Caller".'

'Dark-Caller . . .' Hestor mused. 'I've never heard

that before, though whatever it is, I don't like the sound of it. But the eclipses, and the sixth plane – Yandros and Aeoris, this is starting to make a horrible sort of sense!'

Kitto was baffled, so Hestor did his best to explain about the seven planes that lay between the human world and the realms of the gods.

'The first four planes cause no problems,' he said. 'We – that is, the Circle – work with them all the time, and provided you know the right rituals, the beings that live there are easy enough to control. Then there's the fifth; that's the Plane of Oracles, and the creatures of that realm can be very tricky. Only high-ranking adepts summon them, but provided they protect themselves and use the proper rituals, there isn't any real risk. But then you get to the sixth and seventh planes – and they're another matter entirely.'

The two highest planes, Hestor went on, had never been reached by any adept in living memory, and no adept would be foolhardy enough to try. The beings that lived within these dimensions were extremely dangerous; they were slayers, soul-eaters, and their power, if unleashed, was devastating. One slip, even the tiniest mistake, when performing magic associated with the sixth or seventh plane, and a sorcerer would be destroyed utterly.

'But that's what's so horrifying about Shar's message!' he finished agitatedly. 'If someone could find a way of controlling the beings of those planes, he'd be all but invincible. No one could stand against him. Think about it, Kitto! The double eclipse and the power of the sixth plane – it all ties in with our suspicions about the assassination plot!'

Kitto stared at him. 'That's the perfect time for them to strike; on the night of the eclipse, when the gods' eyes are blinded. That's when they'll try to kill the High Initiate! But what about Shar? What's her part in it?'

'I don't know. But there has to be a connection with her special powers. Thel Starnor must intend to use them in some way. She's in danger, Kitto.'

'This Dark-Caller thing,' Kitto said. 'Maybe that's it? Maybe if we could find out what it means . . .'

Hestor nodded, 'Mother might know, but that council meeting could go on for hours yet.'

'Well, we can't interrupt.' Kitto stood up. 'But if we go down to the entrance hall and wait, we'll see her as soon as she comes out. Come on; its better than sitting here doing nothing.'

They left the room, where Amber was now curled up on Hestor's bed and soundly asleep, and made their way to the main stairs. As they started down they heard a murmur of voices from somewhere below. Hestor leaned over the banisters and his eyes lit as he saw a group of people enter the hallway from the direction of the council chamber.

'The meeting's ended!' With Kitto at his heels he started down the stairs at a run. But in the hall there was no sign of Pellis.

'Where *is* she?' Hestor hissed in frustration.

'Maybe she went upstairs by a back way,' Kitto suggested. 'Or we could try the dining-hall, in case—'

'Hestor? Is something amiss?'

The boys swung round. Standing behind them, with a smile that didn't reflect in his eyes, was Physician Lemor Carrick.

Hestor made a hasty bow, hoping that the physician hadn't seen his consternation before he could mask it. 'No, sir,' he replied. 'We were . . . just looking for my mother.' He started to back away. 'She's probably gone to the dining-hall, so if you'll pardon us . . .'

'To save you the trouble,' Carrick said, 'I'm afraid she isn't there.' He smiled again. 'The High Initiate has just left to begin his vigil before the eclipse, and your mother is among the adepts he has chosen to go with him.'

'Vigil?' Then, to his dismay, Hestor remembered that Neryon Voss's final preparation for the great ritual involved a retreat to a room at the top of one of the castle's four spires. There he and those other adepts who had a major part to play would remain until the eve of the eclipse, spending their time in meditation and prayer as they readied themselves for the task ahead. And no one would be permitted to interrupt them under any circumstances whatever.

Hestor tried to rally his wits. 'I . . . didn't know that Mother had been chosen for the rite,' he said.

'The High Initiate announced his choice at the meeting,' Carrick told him.

'Oh. Oh, yes; I see. Well . . . thank you, sir.'

Carrick regarded him thoughtfully. 'You seemed very anxious to find her. Is there something I can help you with?'

'What? Ah – no, sir. It wasn't very important. Thank you again.'

Carrick nodded, then his gaze slid to Kitto.

'Your ankle seems to have healed well enough, boy. But I'd still advise you not to overdo the running as yet. It will pay you to be cautious.'

The statement seemed to carry an unspoken threat, and the boys felt a chill go through them as they watched Carrick walk away.

13

'Again, Shar. You must memorise the words perfectly. And you must be absolutely sure that you can repeat them without the smallest danger of a mistake.' Thel's voice was relentless and his eyes ice-cold as he stared into Shar's face. 'If you fail, you know what will happen.'

Shar did know, for the threat was like a constant living nightmare to her: You must obey without question. You must learn the ritual, and when the time comes you must perform it flawlessly. You must ensure that nothing goes wrong. For if it does, then the beings of the sixth plane will destroy your soul. Thel had repeated it over and over again since their first confrontation in the cellar, drumming it into her mind like a hideous catechism. For five days now she had striven to learn the movements and gestures and harsh, alien language of the ceremony he was teaching her. She loathed every moment, and the knowledge of what the ritual would lead to made her feel sick to the depths of her heart. But she was too afraid to resist. Whatever the consequences for the High Initiate and for the Circle, she didn't have the strength and courage to sacrifice her own life for their sakes.

For what must have been the twentieth time that day she slowly recited the ritual over again, aware that Thel was listening intently for the slightest error. She didn't even know what the words meant; they were just sounds, guttural and ugly and unclean to her ears. Everything within her screamed a silent protest against uttering them, but, goaded by her fear, she struggled on.

'No, Shar!' Thel's fist slammed down on the table top and his face contorted with anger. 'That phrase is wrong again! How many times must I correct you?'

Shar began to shake. 'I'm trying!' she hissed through clenched teeth. Tears were welling in her eyes.

'Then you must try harder! Once we arrive at the castle there will be no chance for any further rehearsal, and—'

'*What*?'

Thel stopped at her shocked interruption, and Shar realised from his expression that he had inadvertently given away something which he would have preferred her not to hear. Breathing quickly and intently, she said, 'The castle?'

The damage was done and Thel could only make the best of it. He brushed one hand through the air in a careless gesture and replied, 'Very well; it makes no difference whether you learn what you are to do now or later. If you're so eager to know, I will tell you.'

At last, then, Shar understood the final details of the plot as she listened in stunned silence to what

Thel told her. She had presumed that he and his co-conspirators intended to make their attack on Neryon Voss from a distance – but their actual plan was far more audacious. On the night of the double eclipse, Thel said, Circle adepts from every province would gather at the Star Peninsula for the ceremony, and their number would include those who, like himself, had retired from the Circle or moved on to other positions. He and Sister Malia would attend, Shar would go with them, and they would all take their places in the courtyard for the great rite. When the eclipse took place, and the barriers between dimensions were at their weakest, Shar was to speak the words that would summon a sixth-plane entity into the mortal world.

'Neryon Voss will, of course, try to control and banish the creature,' Thel said with cold satisfaction. 'But the eclipse will give the dark forces a far greater power than usual, and even his skills won't be enough to prevail. However, as a Dark-Caller you do have the power to bend those high-plane beings to your will. And you will give the command for the High Initiate's destruction.'

For several seconds then there was silence except for the harsh, rapid sound of Shar's breathing. Then, as if as an afterthought, Thel said smoothly, 'If you think that being at the castle will give you the chance to thwart me, Shar, I'd strongly advise you to forget any such notion. Firstly, I'll ensure that you have no contact with any of your friends. And secondly, if you try to turn the sixth-plane entities against me, you will fail, for the only controlling words you know are those I have taught you. And I don't need to remind you again, do I, of what will happen if you don't follow them exactly?'

Shar looked away and didn't answer. Thel paused a few moments, then nodded.

'I see you understand. Very well; we'll continue with our work. Repeat the ritual once more, from the beginning. And this time, let us have no mistakes!'

She could only obey him. And as she began once again to recite the words, she thought: There is no hope now. I can do nothing to stop this. Neryon Voss will die, and I will be his murderer.

Hestor and Kitto had grasped every chance they could to search the library, but after a day and a half they had still not found what they were looking for. In all the records, ritual-books and histories, it seemed that there was not a single word about a Dark-Caller, and they were beginning to despair. Either this was something so arcane that even the Circle had not documented it, or the cat's telepathic message had been nothing more than garbled nonsense. Pellis or the High Initiate might have known, but both were shut away at the top of the spire and could not be reached. They could trust no one else – and time was rapidly running out.

But then, during the second afternoon of their hunt, their fortunes changed.

They were alone in the library. Hestor had written down the phrase 'Dark-Caller' for Kitto, and the black-haired boy was working his way laboriously through a pile of books to see if he could find any words that looked the same. Three times he had raised Hestor's hopes but had been mistaken, and to relieve his pent-up frustration Hestor was rummaging through some out-of-the-way shelves in a corner, where a jumble of discarded manuscripts lay gathering dust. He didn't expect to find anything, but suddenly a small sheaf of papers tied with a black ribbon caught his eye. It was wedged behind some other documents, and one page tore as he wrestled to pull it out. But at last it came free. And as he looked at the faded, old-fashioned script, Hestor realised that their prayers had been answered.

'Kitto!' He gave such a yell that Kitto started and knocked a book to the floor. 'I've found it – I've found what we need!'

Kitto jumped up and ran to join him. 'Where?' he demanded breathlessly. 'What does it say?'

Hestor stabbed a finger at the first page of the bundle. 'It's a list of the other pages and what they contain. There's an entry for "The skills of the Dark-Caller"!'

'Yandros and Aeoris!' Kitto clutched his arm bruisingly. 'Get the page! Find it!'

Hestor leafed feverishly, then snatched out a single sheet of paper. The writing was spidery and hard to read; squinting, he began to pore over it—

The library door banged and they both jumped as if they had been shot, Kitto turned first, said, 'Oh, gods—' And then Hestor followed his gaze, and froze.

Lemor Carrick stood between them and the door. The physician was staring at them and the look in his eyes was steady, cold and dangerous. Hestor realised that he was holding the document in full view; he made a convulsive move to hide it behind his back but it was too late. Carrick had seen it, and calmly he extended a hand, palm upward.

'Give that to me, if you please, Hestor.'

There was nothing Hestor could do. Fingers shaking, he handed the paper over. The physician glanced at it once, then said, 'And the others.'

Mutely Hestor gave him the sheaf. Carrick knew what they had found; his expression made that intimidatingly clear. And Hestor had no doubt whatever that he also knew why they had been searching for it.

He could hear Kitto breathing harshly and quickly but didn't dare look at him. For several seconds no one moved and the atmosphere in the library built up to a suffocating pitch. Then, very deliberately, the physician slid the paper about the Dark-Caller back into its place in the sheaf, and flexed the sheaf gently between his hands.

'Leave the library,' he said.

A spark of defiance flickered in Hestor's eyes. 'You have no right to order us out!'

'I said, leave the library. And I would advise you, Hestor – I would advise you very strongly – not to probe into matters that are none of your concern. As a physician, I wouldn't recommend it as a healthy occupation.'

Kitto said something foul under his breath, and Hestor went white. 'If you're threatening—'

'Don't be absurd. That is not a threat, it's merely an observation. For your own good.' Carrick stood aside and gestured towards the door. 'Kindly go. Both of you. Now.'

They had no choice. Hestor said savagely, 'Come on, Kitto,' and they strode past Carrick without so much as a glance. The physician shut the door firmly behind them, and the boys trudged up the stairs and out into the courtyard, where Hestor let out his breath in a violent expulsion and leaned against one of the pillars of the covered walkway.

'What fools we were!' He thumped a clenched fist against the black stone. 'One of us should have stood guard!'

'He must have seen us go down there,' Kitto said furiously. 'He knew we were looking for something!'

'Yes; and now he knows what, and probably why as well.' An unpleasant feeling went through Hestor as he recalled how coolly Carrick had revealed his true colours. The physician had made no attempt to dissemble but had openly and carelessly shown them that their suspicions about him were right. Which, to Hestor's mind, could only mean one thing: the plotters were so confident of success that nothing the boys could do or say to anyone would make the slightest difference to their plan.

Kitto spoke up suddenly. 'We'll go back. When Carrick's gone. If we go up to your room we'll be able to see him come out, and then we can look for the paper again.'

Hestor sighed. 'Do you honestly think it'll still be there?'

A pause. 'No.'

'Neither do I; nor anything else that might have helped us. Still, you're right; at least we'll have to look.' Hestor glanced towards the dark, towering finger of the north spire. 'If only the High Initiate hadn't picked Mother to be among the vigil-keepers!'

'Well, he did. So it's up to us to find a way to thwart them, isn't it?'

There was nothing to be said in answer to that. Hestor shrugged, and morosely the two boys set off across the courtyard.

Lemor Carrick left the library half an hour later and, as Hestor and Kitto had guessed, he took the paper from the sheaf with him. In the privacy of his rooms he crumpled the paper into a metal crucible, set light to it, and watched it burn to a small pile of ash. There was a deep frown on his face, and as soon as the last traces of the document had gone he sat down at his table and began to write a letter . . .

* * *

The messenger-bird arrived at the Sisterhood Cot shortly after dark. The Sisters of the Cot believed that Malia had gone into solitary retreat to pray for the High Initiate's wellbeing at the eclipse ritual, and normally the letter the bird carried would have been kept for her return. But the seal marked it as extremely urgent so a servant was despatched to the house in the mountains to deliver it.

Malia took the letter immediately to Thel, and they read it together.

'So.' Thel sat back in his chair, his expression thoughtful. 'Hestor Ennas and that vagabond boy have been busy. What, I wonder, led them to start searching for information about Dark-Callers?'

Malia looked uneasy. 'If they've told Neryon Voss about their suspicions, perhaps he made the connection?' she said.

Thel, however, shook his head. 'I don't think so. Remember, no one else can possibly have fathomed what Shar is, for only we and our friends know that she was born during a double eclipse.' He smiled. 'Lemor Carrick was the attending physician, and he made sure the true time of her birth wasn't entered in the castle records. No; these boys are merely guessing, and it must have been sheer chance that they unearthed that document. I doubt if they have the least idea what it means.'

Malia frowned. 'Unless, of course, Shar's elemental friends have sensed something and communicated with these boys? That's a possibility.'

'True.' Thel paused, then tapped the letter again. 'But elementals' prattling won't be enough to convince the High Initiate. As Carrick says, the boys have no concrete evidence, and without evidence Neryon won't make any move. Believe me, I know him well enough to be certain of that. Besides, however suspicious he might be, he won't deduce the real truth about what we intend to do. That will come as a very great shock.'

They fell silent for a minute or two, both thinking their own thoughts.

Then Thel spoke again. 'All the same, in the light of this perhaps we should take extra care.' He mused for a moment. 'A small safeguard . . . yes, I think that would be wise. And I think I know the ideal way to do it.' He glanced towards the window, to see the position of the first moon. 'Shar should be asleep by now. Come up to her room with me, Malia, please.'

Nonplussed and curious, Malia followed him up the stairs. Shar was indeed asleep, her hair tumbled on her pillow and her face pale and drawn, with heavy shadows beneath her eyes. Thel doused the candle he was carrying, then went to stand by the bed. For a few seconds he gazed down at Shar. The he raised his left hand and moved it, palm down, through the air above her.

Shar stirred and muttered, and Malia saw a faint, glowing aura form around Thel's fingers. There was a sudden heady scent in the air, and Thel's hand moved again, tracing a pattern over the sleeping girl's face. Again Shar stirred, as if trying to escape from a bad dream, and Thel began to speak in a strange, sibilant language. Shar's eyelids fluttered; it seemed she was struggling to wake up, but Thel's power was too great for her – and suddenly her body went limp and very, very still. Thel stopped speaking, and in the quiet he and Malia listened as Shar's breathing became slow and calm and regular.

'She is hypnotised,' Thel said quietly. 'She cannot wake, and she will be unaware of anything that takes place.' He glanced at Malia over his shoulder. 'But let us be certain. Clap your hands.'

Malia did so. Shar didn't react. Malia smiled.

'Good,' Thel said. 'Now I can place her under a much deeper spell which will stay hidden in her mind until and unless it should be necessary to use it. She'll have no knowledge of its presence. But if, at the crucial time, anything should go wrong and she refuses to co-operate, it will be the work of a moment to trigger the command in her subconscious mind. And then she will have no choice but to obey.'

Malia nodded. 'It's a wise precaution. But . . .' she frowned. 'Spells can be broken.'

'That's true. However, I intend to augment this particular magic with something else.' One corner of his mouth curled with chilly satisfaction. 'And when that is done, anyone who tries to break the spell will have a very unpleasant – not to say deadly – surprise in store.'

14

The second moon had risen and its light was filtering in at the window as Hestor and Kitto sat arguing in Hestor's room.

'For the last time, we can't disturb the High Initiate!' Hestor said heatedly. 'To begin with, we wouldn't get near him; there's someone posted by the spire door at all hours. And even if we did, he'd be so furious that he wouldn't give us a chance to explain!'

'So what do we do, then?' Kitto demanded, just as angrily.

Hestor hesitated, and abruptly Kitto saw that he looked very nervous and was clasping his hands so tightly together that the knuckles had turned white.

'You've thought of something!' Kitto's look became intent. 'I know you have, I can see it in your face.'

'Yes,' Hestor said. 'I've thought of something. But I don't think you're going to like it.'

'Can't say until you tell me what it is, can I?'

'All right.' Hestor unclasped his hands, then jammed them together again. He was starting to perspire. 'The only two people in the castle we know we can trust are my mother and Neryon Voss. Anyone else could be in league with Thel and Carrick, and we simply daren't take the risk. Yet at the same time, we desperately need help.'

Kitto made a disparaging noise. 'You're good at stating the obvious!'

'Be quiet and let me finish before you start sneering,' Hestor retorted. 'As I said, we need help. Well, there *is* someone else we can turn to.'

Kitto was taken aback. 'What? Here, in the castle?'

'No. Or at least . . . sort of, but not quite.' Hestor drew a deep breath. 'I don't mean another adept. In fact I don't even mean a human being. I mean someone far greater, who we know we can trust above anything.' He met Kitto's gaze. 'Yandros.'

Kitto stared at him, feeling cold sweat start to break out all over his body. After a few moments, when Hestor didn't speak again, he said softly, 'You're not serious . . .'

'I'm afraid I am. Very serious. I've told you before that Shar and I were both night-born and so dedicated to Chaos rather than Order. I want to conduct a ritual, Kitto. I want to plead to Yandros for help.'

They argued again. Kitto thought the whole idea was madness or blasphemy, or more probably both. Even if they did succeed in calling upon the great lord of Chaos, the chances were that Yandros would annihilate them for their insolence. Hestor snorted at that and said he must be a fool if he thought the gods were that petty, and Kitto retorted that if the gods weren't interested in petty matters, then Yandros couldn't be remotely concerned with their problems. But for all Kitto's objections – and the fears which they were both reluctant to admit to feeling – Hestor was determined, and nothing could sway him. He had no idea at all of how they could call upon the lord of Chaos, for not even the Circle's highest adepts had even attempted to make contact with the gods for many, many years. If there were formal rites that should be performed, he didn't know them and didn't know where to look them up. But, however slender the chances of success, he intended to at least try. Late tonight, when there was no risk of being caught, he would go to the Marble Hall and make his attempt.

'You don't have to come if you don't want to,' he told Kitto. 'If you're too afraid—'

'Afraid?' Kitto interrupted indignantly. 'I'm not afraid! Of course I'll come!'

But for all his bravado, in his heart Kitto felt that they were playing with a deadly fire. And when he looked sidelong at Hestor a few minutes later, he saw that he wasn't alone in having doubts.

As he and Kitto walked soft-footed along the eerily lit passage that led from the library to the Marble Hall, Hestor had uncomfortable memories of his last venture here. Would anything as spectacular happen this time? Or would this whole venture simply be a dismal failure? And though every catechism told him that the gods didn't intervene in mortal affairs, after the bizarre incident in the wake of the Oath Ceremony he couldn't help feeling that Yandros might take an interest in this . . .

As usual, the Marble Hall wasn't locked. Kitto stopped on the threshold, dumbstruck as he stared at the eerie scene of pillars and mists and strange shadows, and when Hestor looked at him he saw that his face had turned white.

'I can't go in here,' Kitto whispered. 'I'm not an adept. It isn't right.'

'Shar isn't an adept either, remember, and she came in here. It's all right, Kitto. You're not breaking any law.' But we are breaking all the rules, Hestor added silently to himself. I just hope that we don't get caught; because this time it would be catastrophe for us both.

He started to move forward into the Hall. Kitto swallowed, hesitated, then slowly followed him. They crossed the mosaic floor to where the seven statues towered silently in the shifting pastel haze, and from the corner of his eye Hestor saw Kitto make a quick bow and spread his fingers in the sign of reverence.

Hestor took up a stance before the central statue and looked up at Yandros's carved face. As they made their way here he had made up a ritual speech of sorts, but suddenly the words deserted him and he couldn't think what to say. He licked dry lips. Kitto was watching him, waiting . . .

Hestor made a low bow to the statue, then closed his eyes and spread his arms wide.

'O Yandros, high lord of Chaos.' His voice came out high-pitched and unsteady; he cleared his throat and started again. 'O Yandros, high lord of Chaos, I stand in this place in humility and reverence, to ask—'

A noise behind him broke his concentration, and Kitto said, 'Oh, no . . .'

Hestor turned round. A few paces away, three cats were staring at him. One was Amber, the other two were from the castle. As he met their gazes they miaowed in chorus, and Amber came forward to rub against his legs.

'How did they get in here?' Hestor asked exasperatedly.

'We must have left the door open.'

'Well, we'd better catch them and put them out, or they'll distract us.'

But the cats wouldn't be caught. Determined to stay, they evaded every effort the boys made to chivvy them out of the Hall, and at last Hestor admitted defeat.

'We'll be here all night at this rate! Come on; we'll simply have to ignore them and hope they don't interrupt us.'

The cats didn't interrupt, but within ten more minutes Hestor knew instinctively that his attempt at a summoning ritual wasn't going to work. The solemn words that he tried to speak didn't ring true to his ears; he couldn't focus his mind well enough to improve on them, and what was intended to be a solemn ceremony crumbled instead into incoherent and frantic pleading. Distractions, too, were creeping in; the knowledge that the cats were staring at him, the small sounds of Kitto fidgeting nervously, the fact that he was perspiring with nervousness himself – it all added up to a recipe for failure.

Then, to make matters worse, they began to bicker. They were both so keyed-up that within seconds tempers had frayed and the small clash was spiralling towards a full-scale argument. Soon they were both shouting, facing each other and gesturing angrily, and echoes of their voices ricocheted around the Marble Hall, adding to the clamour. The ritual was completely forgotten; they had gone too far now to regain their self-control.

Until suddenly, from the direction of the statues, came a sharp, resounding *crack*, like a pane of glass breaking in two.

The boys cut off their argument in appalled shock and, frozen, stared at each other. Kitto's eyes were wide with fright, and Hestor didn't dare look towards the statues. What had they done? Had the noise they were making triggered some unknown force in the Hall? Had they done some terrible damage with their shouting? He felt sick with dread, and his heart was pounding so hard that he thought it would break through his ribs at any moment. He *had* to look at the statues. Somehow, he had to find the courage. Slowly, so very slowly, Hestor forced himself to turn his head.

There was a shadow by the central statue, and he knew it had not been there before. Then, like a dark wing, it moved . . .

Hestor's stomach lurched and he grabbed Kitto's arm, making a strangled noise. Kitto, too, began to turn—

And from the shadow, moving with lithe grace, a tall figure stepped out into the Marble Hall.

Golden hair flowed over his narrow shoulders, framing a bony, hawklike face which was proud, sinister, knowing and humorous all at once. He was dressed simply, almost carelessly, in the kind of clothes that any castle-dweller might have worn, but there were writhing tongues of fire in his cloak, and a dark aura burned around him. And when Hestor, unable to stop himself, met the gaze of his slanting eyes, he saw them change colour from green to crimson to the pewter-grey of a threatening storm-sky.

At his side Kitto uttered a tiny, horrified whimper. He knew the truth. They both knew. Neither of them needed to look again at the stone statue, and terror rooted them to the floor.

They were confronting a power that no living adept had ever encountered. For Yandros of Chaos had answered their call.

Yandros turned his head fractionally, and his gaze raked the boys in turn, seeming to strip them to the core of their souls. Kitto had started to tremble like a leaf and Hestor's head spun with panic-stricken pressure. What had he done? Kitto had said they were playing with fire – dear gods he was right, and now the fire was going to burn them!

Suddenly Amber gave a cry. The sound shattered the rising tension, and through the shocked daze that it left in its wake Hestor saw the three cats run past him to the lord of Chaos, their tails raised high. Yandros noticed them. He laughed – and bewilderedly Hestor heard that the laugh was gentle, affectionate, amused. And Yandros was extending a graceful hand to Amber, crouching to stroke him while Amber purred loudly. The other cats pushed in, thrusting their heads against Yandros's arm, and Hestor remembered the great affinity that cats were said to have with the powers of Chaos. It was possible, he thought with an inward shudder, just possible, that the cats had turned the tide in their favour.

But then Yandros straightened and looked at the boys again, and Hestor's tiny flame of confidence was snuffed out. He tried desperately to hold the god's gaze but it was impossible, for those unhuman eyes were searing him and he had no defence against them. And their colour had changed now to black.

'Hestor. Kitto.' Yandros's voice was serene and mellifluous – but it had an extremely dangerous edge. 'I presume you have a good reason for breaking one of the Circle's most fundamental rules by doing what you have done? To make an appeal to the powers of Chaos is a privilege reserved only for a very few mortals in this world.'

Hestor's fear abruptly redoubled. He dropped to one knee – Kitto was already kneeling and had covered his face with his hands – and said unsteadily, 'Lord Yandros . . . I . . . .' Yandros waited, one eyebrow raised in faint query, but Hestor couldn't continue. Miserably he shook his head, staring at the floor.

'I see.' Yandros said. 'So it was simply an exercise in disobedience, was it? A childish game, with no purpose?'

'No, my lord! It wasn't—'

Then Hestor stopped as he saw the faint, wry smile on Yandros's face. The god's eyes changed to a peculiar purplish-blue and he said less sternly, 'Ah, so you *do* have a purpose, but you're afraid to admit it to me.' His dark aura pulsed with energy and Hestor felt a slow, soundless throbbing begin somewhere deep under the Marble Hall's floor. 'One lesson you should learn, Hestor, is that we of Chaos are more likely to censure you for dissembling than for being truthful.' He paused. 'And there's no need to kneel before me; it's a habit I have no time for. Get up, both of you.'

They did, though nervously, and Yandros nodded. 'That's better. Now: you seem to believe that this is an emergency which justifies your flouting all you have been taught. You are in no position to judge that, and to think you are is both arrogant and naive.'

Hestor quailed, but the lord of Chaos continued with a mellowed voice. 'However, I think in this case the offence might be pardonable. The summoning you performed was inept and most certainly not worthy of a Circle-trained adept, but it was sincere. You are both extremely agitated, and I see that you have a very deep belief in what you are trying to do. That makes me curious – tell me your story.'

For the first time since Yandros's appearance Hestor and Kitto dared to look at each other, and both saw the glimmer of hope in each other's eyes. Yandros, it seemed, was as capricious and unpredictable as all the old tales maintained. He would act on a whim, and, against all the odds, their predicament had intrigued him. Kitto nodded fractionally, encouraging Hestor to speak. Hestor licked his lips, trying to pluck up courage, and Yandros said mildly, 'I am interested, Hestor, but my patience has limits.' Abruptly the mists of the Hall thickened and swirled, and through them the god's face looked ominous. 'Speak.'

So, haltingly and with a good deal of nudging and whispering from Kitto, Hestor told their entire story, including the tale of Amber's garbled message to them, which could only have come directly from Shar. When he heard this Yandros held up a hand, stopping Hestor in mid-sentence, and turned to look at the ginger cat again. The pupils of Amber's eyes dilated and he gave voice to a long yowl.

'Peace, little one,' Yandros said gently. 'I understand your thoughts.' The he turned to the boys once more. 'A Dark-Caller. Do you know what that means?'

'No, my lord,' Hestor replied unhappily. 'But we think it must have some connection with Shar.'

Yandros nodded, and his expression grew serious. 'It has. Shar is a Daughter of Storms, as you already know, but she also has another birthright, and one that is potentially very dangerous. When she was born there was an eclipse of both moons, just as there will be in a few days from now.'

Hestor was startled. 'There was no mention of that in the records!'

'No. Someone, it seems, had a good reason to hide it, and clearly that person knew Shar's value.' Yandros's eyes turned the colour of bronze. 'Children born during an eclipse of sun or moons have particular powers which other mortals can't command. They have the ability to summon and control the beings which inhabit the higher elemental planes – beings which owe no allegiance whatever to the gods.'

'The ritual that the High Initiate is preparing for . . .' Hestor said. 'It's to keep such creatures at bay.'

'Precisely. During an eclipse, the gateways between this dimension and the elemental planes become blurred, and the higher entities find it easier to enter this world. Which, as your Circle studies should have taught you,' Yandros smiled dryly, 'they will do if they can, for they relish preying on the energies and even the souls of mortals. At such times, a Dark-Caller's powers can be invaluable . . . for good or for ill.'

For the first time since Yandros had materialised in the Marble Hall, Kitto dared to speak. 'And Shar is . . . one of these Dark-Callers?' he whispered in awe.

'She is the first Caller to be born in the human world for more than a hundred years,' Yandros told him. 'By rights – and especially as an adept's daughter – she should have been brought up in the castle and trained to use her abilities properly. Clearly, though, someone had other plans for her.'

'The same someone who altered the castle records?' Hestor asked.

Yandros gave him an enigmatic look. 'Surmise that for yourself, Hestor. Though I suspect you've already answered the question in your own mind.'

Hestor had, and it chilled him. All the threads tied together now, from the motive behind Shar's kidnap right back to the deaths of her parents, which he was now convinced had been plain murder. Suddenly and desperately he looked at Yandros. 'What are they going to do with her, my lord?' he pleaded. 'You can see into mortal minds and hearts – you surely must know what their plan is!'

To his dismay, however, Yandros shook his head,

the flames in his cloak flickering darkly. 'If you believe the gods are omnipotent, Hestor, then you have a great deal to learn!' he said. 'I do not know the inner thoughts of mortal, and nor can I watch every small event that takes place in this world. Like you, I can only speculate on what the plotters intend. But clearly they mean to attack the High Initiate during the eclipse, when the barrier between this world and the elemental planes is at its weakest. It seems likely that they will call a sixth-plane elemental to do their work for them, and use Shar as their medium.'

A feeling of dread was creeping through Hestor's marrow. 'What will happen to Shar, my lord?' he whispered. 'What will such a thing do to her?'

'It is possible that she will come through unscathed,' Yandros replied. Then his eyes changed colour again, this time to a cold, acid green. 'But it is also unlikely. Without the full training that she should have had, she will be vulnerable, and if the slightest thing goes amiss she will probably die.'

'Gods—' Hestor quickly made the sign of reverence. 'Forgive me, lord Yandros, I meant no disrespect, but—' His fists clenched and suddenly words burst from him in a flood. 'Please, my lord, *please*, you must help us! We can't stand by and let this happen; it's unjust, it's hideous, it's so wrong! Please, lord Yandros, you can stop it if you will! Save Shar and the High Initiate, and punish these criminals!'

'No, Hestor,' Yandros said sternly. 'I will not.'

'But—'

'I said, *no*.' The tone silenced Hestor. Then Yandros relented a little and his look became kinder. 'As a Circle initiate, you shouldn't need reminding that we of Chaos, like our cousins in the realm of Order, do not interfere in mortal affairs.'

Hestor shook his head miserably. 'I don't understand, my lord! All our teachings say that the gods protect the world against evil powers, so surely—'

'Evil powers, Hestor, are not the same thing as evil men,' Yandros said severely. 'Besides, as my cousin Aeoris of Order would be the first to tell you,' – now his mouth curled in a cynical smile – 'the definition of evil depends entirely on the direction from which you view it. But that's not relevant here; what matters is that while we do watch over the world at large, and our power shields mortals from certain forces that might otherwise do great harm, where human matters are concerned you must solve your own problems as best you can, without help from us.' He paused, regarding Hestor detachedly. 'Do you understand me now?'

Hestor's shoulders drooped. He did understand, and though everything inside him railed against it, he knew he must accept. Bitterly he remembered Kitto's comment that the gods wouldn't be remotely interested in their petty problems, and inwardly he acknowledged that the black-haired boy had been right. He had risked his entire future by doing what he had done tonight. And it had all been for nothing.

'Hestor,' Yandros spoke again. Slowly Hestor

looked up, and saw that the lord of Chaos was still watching him. Yandros's eyes were silver now, and his aura cast eerie shadows over his face and form. The flames in his cloak had subsided to glowing embers.

'You think there is nothing you can do,' Yandros said. 'But there is – or might be, if you and Shar are prepared to take even the smallest chance that comes your way.'

Hestor's expression grew cautiously hopeful. 'My lord?'

'Remember that as well as being a Dark-Caller, Shar is also a Daughter of Storms,' Yandros continued. 'She has an affinity with the Warps, as you discovered for yourselves not long ago. And the Warps, of course, are under our control.' Now a faint smile was playing around his mouth. 'The outcome of this little intrigue is of no direct concern to me . . . but I am in an indulgent mood at the moment. I won't give you any direct help, but I will grant you – or rather, Shar – one small favour; simply as an acknowledgement of her birthright. Tonight Shar will have a dream. If she remembers it on waking she will understand how to use the power of the Warps to aid her.'

Hestor's pulse quickened. 'The Warps? How can she—?'

'No questions,' Yandros cut across warningly. 'How, and even if, she uses what I will grant her is entirely for her to decide. The remedy is in her hands, just as the High Initiate's salvation, or otherwise, is in the hands of himself and his friends.

You must all succeed or fail on your own merits.'

Dry-mouthed, Hestor nodded. 'Yes, lord Yandros. Th-thank you.'

Yandros raised a sardonic eyebrow. 'I'm glad to see you don't neglect the basic courtesies. But your thanks are neither here not there to me. Leave the Marble Hall now. You've stirred up more than enough for one night. And if you repeat this flagrant venture, don't be so foolish as to think that I will answer you a second time.'

Both boys flushed to the roots of their hair but didn't have the confidence to reply. They heard a soft sound, like the swish of a heavy curtain. A shadow moved across the Marble Hall, darkening the mists momentarily. And Yandros was gone.

15

Shar woke with a jolt, and opened her eyes to be confronted by brilliant light. She winced, shrinking away, and in an instant the light faded to a cool, silvery gloom. It was not full day as she had first thought; in fact dawn hadn't yet broken, and the last rays of the waning second moon were trickling in at the window, casting dim, gaunt shadows across her bed.

What, then, was that vivid glare? Shar was still hazy with sleep, but something was lurking at the back of her mind; the sense of a dream suddenly interrupted. She remembered a golden colour . . . someone's hair? Hestor had fair hair, but this had been far brighter; a molten flare like living fire. And it was important. On a deep-rooted, intuitive level Shar knew it was vitally important. As though someone had been transmitting a message to her while she slept . . .

She pushed back the covers, got out of bed and went to the window to stare out. Every instinct in her was yearning to push aside the bars and break free into the sweet, clean air of the mountains. Had that, too, been part of her dream? She must remember!

She tried a mental exercise she had learned during her first days at the Sisterhood Cot, to bring back the details of dreams half forgotten. At first she thought it wasn't going to work, but after a few minutes new images began to form in her mind. Golden hair, yes; and the hair framed a face which was strange, beautiful, almost unhuman . . . and which she had seen before. Who was it? Those slanting eyes and fine, almost razor-sharp bones were familiar! Yet a name wouldn't come. But she knew in her marrow that this face was not the face of any ordinary mortal.

And she remembered that in the dream his lips had moved, and his voice had spoken to her. Just one word, but repeated over and over again: *Escape. Escape. Escape.*

A shudder ran through Shar as she felt the powerful urgency of that word. It was almost a command, and one she desperately wanted to obey. But how? *How*?

Suddenly, and so quickly that her consciousness almost didn't catch it, another image flicked through her mind, sending a tingle down her spine. A huge, dim wheel of dark colours, turning slowly in the sky . . . had a Warp storm been part of her dream? She couldn't recall, but, again, it seemed important.

Shar found that she was gripping the bars of the window, her hands clenched so tightly on them that her knuckles were turning white. The second moon had vanished now and the sky was streaked with faint dawn light. Below her she could see the tangle of the garden and she realised abruptly that the bar under her left hand was loose.

She gave a sharp tug, and a small shower of rubble scattered to the floor. The bar wobbled, and a heady mixture of astonishment and hope began to rise within her. If she could only pull the bar right out, the gap it left would be just large enough for her to squeeze through! And the wall outside the window was covered with a vine whose stems looked strong enough to bear her weight.

Feverishly Shar began to tug at the bar again. But although it was by now very loose, it wouldn't come free. She shut her eyes, clenching her teeth with effort, and her lips formed frantic, urgent words.

'Gods, grant me strength! Yandros and all the lords of Chaos, please help me now!' She was rocking backwards and forwards on her feet, pulling with all the energy she could muster. Then with no warning there was a squeal, a grating noise, more rubble fell, and the bar dropped to the floor with a metallic clatter.

Shar stumbled backwards, almost losing her balance, and her eyes snapped wide open. She had done it! Whether the gods had answered her plea, or whether she had found the strength from the depths of her own will, she didn't know; but she had the chance she had craved so desperately – the chance to escape!

Eagerly she ran back to the window, but abruptly froze as she heard a sound from the room below. Someone else was up and about, and moments later she heard the noise of the garden door opening. Shar pressed herself against the wall and peered down in time to see Sister Malia come into view. She walked a few paces into the garden, then stopped and stood gazing at the lightening sky, her shoulders rising and falling as she breathed in the cool, fresh air. Shar had forgotten Malia's habit of taking an early-morning walk, and realised how easily she could have run into disaster. Two more minutes and Malia would have caught her climbing down the vine . . . perspiration prickled her skin and she gave silent thanks for her narrow escape. Now she would have to wait until Malia went back into the house, and pray in the meantime that she didn't look up and see the tell-tale gap in the bars.

Minutes crawled by while Shar crouched watching at the window, trying to control her racing nerves. Malia seemed to be taking for ever over her walk, and with the daylight growing brighter all the time Shar knew that her chances of fleeing unnoticed were becoming slimmer and slimmer. But at last, to her enormous relief, Malia turned back towards the house. She paused one last time to survey the morning, and Shar heard her give a little huff of satisfaction. Then she disappeared inside, and the sound of the door shutting echoed in the valley.

Shar jumped up, peeled off her nightgown and scrambled into outdoor clothes. She was almost daunted when she swung one leg over the windowsill and looked at the drop below. If she fell, she would at very least break several bones. But the vine looked strong. And as a child, she had climbed plenty of trees and creeper-covered walls in the High Margrave's garden on Summer Isle. She could do it, she told herself determinedly. She *had* to do it.

She leaned out and gripped a thick stem of the vine. It pulled away from the wall a little but then held, and cautiously Shar eased herself out of the window. Finding the first foothold was hard, but at last she wedged her toes into the fork of a branch. Then, with a wild, silent prayer, she trusted her entire weight to the vine.

There was a creak and a violent rustling, and to her horror the branch she was gripping started to tear away from the wall. An old memory came to her rescue and she let herself slide down until she reached an area that was still secure. Move quickly, that was the secret – the vine wouldn't bear her weight for long and the faster she could scramble down, the safer she would be. She took a deep breath, renewed her grip, and started to half climb and half slither through the leaves. The vine groaned alarmingly and twigs snapped off beneath her feet; again the branch she was holding started to pull away from the wall, and again she scrabbled haphazardly down to a safer section. A quick glance told her that she was more than halfway to the ground, and her spirits soared. Another arm's length and she could jump the rest!

Shar made the last, breathless descent in seconds, then twisted around and sprang to make a soft landing among neglected shrubs. Her arms and legs were scratched, there were leaves in her hair, and she had scraped two fingers of one hand as she slid down. But none of that mattered. She was free.

The garden door was no more than five paces from where she had landed, but now that Malia had had her morning walk Shar didn't expect any more danger from that quarter. And she was too elated at gaining her freedom for the sound of footsteps behind the door to register in her mind. So it came as a terrible shock, as she struggled out of the shrubs and gained her feet, to see the door open and Sister Malia appear on the threshold.

For a paralysing second they stared at each other, Shar horrified and Malia astounded. Then Malia recovered her wits, and her voice rang in shrill alarm.

'Thel! Come quickly! She's escaping!'

As she cried out she made a lunge for Shar and, driven by a frantic reflex, Shar whirled round and bolted like a frightened cat across the garden. She heard Malia running after her, heard her furious command to 'Come back, come back!' but she didn't dare look round to see if the Sister was gaining on her. The wall was directly ahead, she was racing towards it – but then, to her horror, she realised that it was too high for her to scramble up and over. She would be trapped!

Shar swerved aside, breath sawing in her throat. Where was the gate? There must be one, she must have come through it when she was brought here; but she couldn't remember! Then another door banged somewhere, and on the edge of her vision she saw a second figure appear. *Thel.* He was running from the far side of the house, she could hear him shouting, and if she kept on her present course she would cannon straight into him! Again she swerved, ploughing across the softer soil of what had once been a vegetable patch – and she didn't see the long, whippy briar stem that snaked across her path until suddenly her foot tangled in it.

She was jerked off balance, felt thorns tearing at her ankle, and with a yell of startled pain she spun round, performing a helpless dance as she strove not to fall. She didn't fall, but the precious few seconds it took to extricate herself were enough for Malia to catch up. With a triumphant cry the Sister pounced, grabbing one of Shar's arms and wrenching her round. Twisting, Shar bit Malia's hand with all her strength. Malia squealed, Shar felt her grip loosen, and she broke free, sprinting in a new direction. And suddenly there was the gate ahead of her, down a short section of paved path! If she could only reach it before Thel did—

Every muscle and sinew in Shar's body strained with renewed effort as she tried to increase her pace. But suddenly she couldn't see properly; the daylight seemed to be dimming, there was a singing in her ears, and panic hit her – *what was happening to her?*

Was she going to faint? Something had gone wrong with the sky . . .

Then in a stunning instant her flailing mind realised the truth. The sky was changing! And the singing in her ears came from outside, from all around her, and it was growing louder, turning to a piercing scream.

Shar heard Malia cry out in alarm but the Sister's voice was almost drowned by the swelling noise from the heavens. There was a sound like a detonation far, far away, and a blast of wind roared across the garden, buffeting in Shar's face and setting her hair streaming out like a banner. Then the sky split apart as crimson lightning turned the scene into mayhem, and through the stunning glare Shar saw the huge, ghostly bands of colour – purple and violet and blood-red and bronze and a dark, baleful green – that were starting to wheel slowly across the sky as the Warp storm came sweeping out of the north.

She skidded to a halt, stunned into immobility by the battering assault on her senses. Lightning tore across the sky a second time, and the shrill scream was merging with new sounds; eerie wailings and eldritch harmonies, as the Warp found its full voice.

'Shar! Shar!' Above the din she heard Thel bellowing. 'You can't escape us now! Don't be a fool – get into the house before the storm strikes!'

His cry snapped Shar's trance and she whirled round to see that he and Malia were running towards her. Behind her was the gate, and with a gasp she spun again and flung herself towards it. Her hands closed, scrabbling, on the latch; she pulled – but it was locked, the key was not there. She was trapped!

'Shar!' Thel yelled again. 'It's no use! Get to shelter!'

And, on the heels of his furious command, another voice, a voice from her dream, echoed in Shar's head.

Escape . . . Escape . . . There was triumph in the voice; triumph and a colossal sense of power. And in that instant Shar understood what the dream had meant.

'No!' She shrieked the word at Thel and Malia as they rushed at her through the storm's confusion. 'No! I won't give in to you!' With a violent movement she flung her arms skywards, and her voice rose in a prayer, a plea, a command to the supernatural storm. She felt a huge surge of energy that seemed to rip her mind in half; she heard a roar that eclipsed every other sound in the world. Like a gargantuan wall of noise and light and power, the Warp swept over her, and as Thel reeled back, yelling out in fury and frustration, Shar vanished into the mayhem of the storm.

Shar regained consciousness to find herself lying face down on rough ground. Her forehead and one cheek were grazed, and her hands too, as if she had tried to save herself from falling. But she could remember nothing of that. Her last recollection was of being snatched away by the Warp only an instant before

Thel would have recaptured her, and everything since that moment was a blank in her mind.

Slowly she sat up, wondering where the supernatural storm had carried her this time. To her surprise – and dismay – she saw high rock walls towering to either side of her, and realised that once again she was in the mountains, on a road winding through a long, narrow pass. Shar shaded her eyes and gazed all around, hoping to see some familiar landmark, but in surroundings like this one stretch of road looked very much like any other, and it was impossible to judge whether she had been here before.

She climbed cautiously to her feet. Luckily she seemed to have no injuries apart from the grazes, but her clothes were filthy and the heel of one shoe had broken. She was trying to wedge it back on when a sound alerted her – the clattering hoofbeats of several horses, beyond the next curve and approaching rapidly. Shar's heart lurched as she remembered the brigand attack, and, as best she could with the broken shoe, she started to make for a nearby rock outcrop where she could hide until the danger, if there was danger, had passed.

She wasn't swift enough, however, and before she could conceal herself the leading horses appeared round the curve. There was a shout of surprise as the riders saw her, then a voice called out a command to halt. And Shar stood staring at six mounted men and women who all wore the gold badges of Circle adepts.

'Fourteen gods, what's this?' The riders' leader took in Shar's dishevelled state and horrified expression, and slid down from his saddle. 'Child, are you all right? What are you doing here?'

Shar realised that she had never met any of these people before, so even if one of them was in league with Thel the chances of her being recognised were slender. Relief flooded over her in a dizzy wave and on its heels came the knowledge that the riders could be an answer to her most fervent prayers.

'Oh, please,' she said, stumbling to meet the adept, 'can you help me? I was travelling with my parents to the Star Peninsula, but—'

'Did you get caught in the Warp?' the adept interrupted anxiously.

'Yes – yes, we did.' Grateful for the lead he had unwittingly given her, Shar latched on to the idea. 'We tried to find shelter, but my horse panicked and bolted. It must have galloped for miles, then I was thrown, and now I'm lost!'

The other adepts had dismounted by this time and they gathered round. They too were on their way to the castle, they said, to attend the eclipse ceremony, and they asked Shar sympathetic questions. Where, exactly, had her party been on the road when the Warp struck? Which direction had her horse taken when it bolted? Did she know how much time had passed since she and her parents had become separated? For safety's sake Shar gave vague answers, and when asked her name she said it was Fiora. She pretended to be confused and upset, and the adepts were kindly; they too had been caught unawares by the Warp and had been hard pressed to keep together when it swept over them.

'Horses don't have much sense where Warps are concerned,' the leader said with a rueful laugh. 'If we hadn't managed to control ours, our party would have been scattered over a five-mile radius by now! Don't worry, Fiora, we'll get you back to your parents.'

'They've probably ridden on to the castle to get help,' a dark-haired woman said reassuringly. 'We might even meet a search party on the road.'

'That's true. Anyway, we're only a few hours from the Star Peninsula, so we'll soon find out. Come on, Fiora – you can ride pillion with Vetke, and we'll be on our way.'

'Don't worry, my dear,' Vetke said with a reassuring smile. 'You're safe now. There's no more danger.'

Shar returned her smile. But silently, wryly, she thought: If only you knew how wrong you are.

16

Shar and her rescuers reached the Star Peninsula at noon. For all its dizzying terrors, Shar thought that the rock bridge to the castle was the most welcome sight she had ever seen, and as the horses clattered under the barbican arch and into the courtyard, she sent a silent prayer of relief and gratitude to all fourteen of the gods.

'Well, Fiora,' the woman called Vetke said kindly, 'we'd best inquire quickly for your parents. If—'

'Shar!' A shout from across the courtyard interrupted the woman, and Shar swung round to see Hestor, his face lit by incredulous delight, running towards her.

She turned to Vetke. 'It's Hestor – my . . . my cousin.'

'I thought he called you—' Vetke began, puzzled, but before she could say any more Shar called out hastily to the approaching boy, praying that he would take his cue from her.

'Hestor, it's all right, I'm safe! We got separated during the Warp. Have Mother and Father arrived, and is Aunt Pellis here?'

Despite his shock at seeing her, Hestor had the wit to realise that she had invented a tale. 'Ah – yes, yes, all's well,' he replied; then, 'What happened?'

In a few sentences Shar told him of her rescue in the mountains and Hestor bowed respectfully to the adepts' leader. 'Thank you, sir! My mother – Pellis Bradow Ennas; I'm sure you know her – will be so relieved to see Cousin Shar safe!'

'Cousin Fiora,' Shar said quickly. 'You always confuse me with my twin, don't you, Hestor?'

'Uh . . . yes, I do, don't I?' Hestor smiled pallidly and made another bow. 'Thank you again, sirs and ladies. With your permission I'll take Sha— Fiora to her parents straight away.'

The adepts smiled permission, though still a little bemusedly, and taking Shar's arm Hestor hurried her away.

And from an upper window Physician Lemor Carrick, alerted by the new arrivals, drew his brows together in an ominous frown as he watched their progress across the courtyard.

In the sanctuary of Pellis's apartments confusion reigned for some time as Shar, Hestor and Kitto all tried to tell their stories at once. There was so much to explain, and all of it so momentous, that it was hard to untangle the threads; and the attentions of Amber and three of the castle cats added to the disarray. But at last everything was told – and the boys' elation at Shar's escape vanished as the extreme urgency of the situation came fully home to them.

Shar's tale, as Hestor grimly said, confirmed all that Yandros had told them in the Marble Hall. The worst of it was that they would have no chance to warn the High Initiate – or Pellis – of the danger until the spire retreat was over. And that wouldn't happen until the eve of the eclipse.

'So there are no friends we can turn to,' Shar said uneasily.

'No. But there are enemies,' Kitto put in, his blue eyes fierce. 'Or at least one – that crawler of a physician. If he should find out that you're here, you won't be safe.' He glanced sidelong at the other boy. 'And neither will Hestor.'

Hestor, though, shook his head. 'No, Kitto, you're wrong. Thel won't have me harmed. He only threatened it to force Shar to co-operate, and now that she's no longer in his hands, killing me wouldn't achieve anything.' He paused. 'Mind you, he might well try another tactic, such as ordering his accomplices to take one of us hostage.'

Shar shivered, and Kitto said ferociously, 'I know how to handle a knife – I'll made sure that doesn't happen to any of us!'

Hestor turned to Shar. 'You'd best stay in Mother's room; that's probably the safest place. And if Kitto's as good as he says with a knife, he can guard us all.'

For the moment it seemed there was nothing they could do, and with an effort they turned their minds to more basic matters. First and foremost was some food for Shar, who had eaten nothing since the previous evening. Kitto volunteered to go to the dining-hall and bring something back, and when he had gone Shar was thankful simply to sink into a chair and close her eyes as weariness washed over her.

But the respite lasted less than a minute before pounding footsteps announced Kitto's headlong return.

'It's Carrick!' Kitto slammed the door at his back and gasped the words out. 'I've just seen him in the corridor – he's coming this way!'

Hestor jumped to his feet. 'If he suspects anything—'

'He'll push his way in here and he'll see Shar!' Kitto finished the sentence for him. 'Shar, you've got to hide!'

'Where?' Shar was white-faced. 'If he is suspicious he'll search these rooms and you won't be able to stop him!'

'Get out of the apartments,' Hestor said. 'Quickly, before Carrick—'

Kitto interrupted. 'It's too late for that; he'll be in sight by now! There's got to be somewhere . . .'

Suddenly Shar knew that she only had one chance. She said nothing – the boys would have argued, and there was no time to argue – but ran to the window and flung it open. By the time Hestor and Kitto realised what she intended, she had already scrambled up on to the sill, and their eyes widened with horror.

'Shar, no!' Hestor cried. 'You'll fall, you'll kill yourself!'

He and Kitto ran towards her, determined to drag her back by force if necessary, and the cats set up an agitated noise. But Shar had no intention of trying to climb on to the outside ledge as they feared. She had another idea – and the boys had forgotten her affinity with elementals. They heard her call out, a high-pitched, frantic cry that was part command and part plea. And an instant later a huge gust of air slammed through the room, sending them reeling backwards. Arms flailing, gasping with shock, they saw the gust whip into a small whirlwind filled with spectral faces, clutching hands, fluttering, filmy wings. Like a tiny storm the air elementals materialised around Shar; they caught hold of her fingers, her arms, her dress, and with a second enormous gust they whisked her out of the window and away upwards.

Hestor and Kitto ran to the window and were about to lean out, striving to see where Shar had been taken, when the sharp sound of the door opening behind them made them jump back.

Lemor Carrick walked into the room. The boys spun round and at the sight of their expressions Carrick's own face hardened suspiciously.

Struggling to sound nonchalant, Hestor said, 'Good day, sir. Is there something I can do for you?'

Carrick regarded him through narrowed eyes. 'You mother borrowed a book from me some while ago, Hestor. I need it back, so I'm here to fetch it.'

'A book?' Hestor frowned. 'I haven't seen it, sir, so I don't know where it is. When Mother returns from the vigil, I'll ask her to return it to you.'

'I'm afraid it can't wait until then; I need to have it now. I'm sure your mother would have no objection to my finding it for myself.'

'Of course. You're very welcome.'

Carrick hadn't expected Hestor to agree so easily, but he masked his chagrin and started to search. As he went through each room he made a show of looking in all the obvious places where books might be found, but Hestor and Kitto noticed that he also looked in un-obvious places – in cupboards, behind curtains, even under beds. He was clearly baffled and angry to find no trace of Shar, and at last said stiffly that as the book was not to be found he would not trouble them any further. Exchanging relieved grins behind his back, Hestor and Kitto escorted him to the outer door.

And then Carrick stopped as his gaze lit on something none of them had noticed before. A pair of girl's shoes, one with a broken heel, lying at the foot of a chair.

He said nothing. He simply gave the boys just one look, over his shoulder, and smiled a contemptuous, triumphant smile. Then he walked out of the apartments and away along the corridor.

Hestor groaned and subsided on to another chair. 'Fools we are – we didn't even see them there!'

Kitto picked up the shoes and shoved them out of sight, though the damage was done now. 'They could have been anyone's shoes,' he said hopefully. 'Your mother's for instance.'

'Mother wouldn't wear shoes like those, and Carrick knows it. Besides, you saw that smile. He knows Shar's here and he knows we're hiding her.' Hestor sighed heavily. 'The only thing to be thankful for is that he doesn't know exactly where she is.'

Kitto blinked rapidly. 'Come to that, neither do we! Where did the elementals take her?'

In the small crisis of the shoes Hestor had completely forgotten about Shar herself, and he jumped to his feet, shocked. Again they ran to the window, but when they leaned precariously out and looked upwards there was nothing to be seen but the castle wall and the sky.

'The roof!' Hestor said, ducking back in again. 'There's a stairway that leads up – come on, we'll see better from there!'

They raced out, away along the passage and into a smaller corridor that led to the rooftop stairs. And halfway up the flight, they met Shar coming down.

'Shar!' Hestor cried. 'Where were you? Where did the elementals carry you?'

'To the battlements!' Shar's hair was windblown and her cheeks pink with breathlessness and the rush of her ascent. 'Then they kept watch for me and told me when Carrick had gone.' She paused. 'Does he suspect?'

'More than that; he knows,' Hestor said, and told her about the shoes. 'But it makes little difference; Thel has probably already scried to find you, so he must have a good idea of where you are.'

She sighed. 'We'll just have to be extremely careful.'

'And watch for any sign of trouble,' Kitto added. 'Hestor, when will your mother and the High Initiate return?'

'If the gods are with us,' Hestor said, 'it should be tomorrow evening.'

'Pray they are with us, then,' said Kitto. 'Because if they're not, I don't give much for our chances of keeping Thel and Carrick at bay for long.'

With Kitto going ahead to check that all was clear they walked back to the apartments. They locked the door behind them and Hestor cast a simple watching-spell which, in theory, should alert them if Carrick or anyone else came prying; though, as he said wryly, he didn't have the skill or experience to guarantee that it would work.

He was just completing it when Kitto, who had been staring out of the window said, 'There's a messenger-bird leaving.' Shar went to look and he added, 'Care to bet about who sent it?'

She nodded. 'Carrick. Well, even if my uncle doesn't yet know where I am, he soon will.' Then her face took on an introverted look. 'We know he won't give up, but as to what he *will* do . . . I truly can't guess, Kitto. I truly can't.'

'Well,' Kitto said, 'we'll find out soon enough.' He tried to force a smile but it didn't quite work. 'Three days from now we'll know, won't we? One way or the other, it'll be settled.'

'Yes,' she said bleakly. 'Yes, it will . . .'

To Sister Malia's surprise, Thel wasn't unduly alarmed by the news from Physician Carrick. From the very beginning he had known that if Shar escaped she would try to reach the castle, and he had made his plans accordingly. Yes, in one sense it was a setback. But the arrangements they had already made would not need to change.

'We will leave for the castle as planned,' he told Malia. 'And when we arrive, we will behave as if nothing whatever is amiss.'

Malia stared at him in astonishment. 'But Shar will have told Neryon Voss everything!' she protested. 'We'll be arrested on sight.'

'You're wrong, my dear,' said Thel with a cool smile. 'Neryon Voss will do nothing, for whatever he might believe, he can't be certain of the truth. Remember, the only evidence against us is the testimony of Shar and that junior initiate Hestor, and, as I've said before, I know Neryon well enough to be sure that he won't act on that alone. No, Malia; I assure you we'll be perfectly safe.'

Malia accepted that, though uneasily, and said, 'But then there's the matter of Shar herself. Even if the High Initiate is unsure about her story, he'll take precautions. To begin with, we won't be allowed near her – in fact he'll probably pretend that she isn't at the castle, but will keep her hidden. And what will happen if he should discover the hypnotic command that you've placed in her mind?'

'Discovering it is one matter, but erasing it will be quite another,' Thel replied. 'He'll soon realise that any attempt to meddle with that particular spell will endanger Shar's life and he won't put her at risk. Similarly, if he keeps her hidden from us that, too, presents no problem, for I can trigger the command in Shar's mind no matter where she is. In fact . . .' He paused, considering, then a chilly smile spread across his face. 'In fact, I'm beginning to think that this new situation is to our advantage.'

'How can that be?' Malia asked dubiously.

Thel's smile grew broader. 'Neryon Voss is a logical man. If Shar has told him everything she knows, he will anticipate the attack – if it comes – at a certain point in the eclipse ritual. I, however, have a different plan. The attack will not come at a logical moment, and nor will it take the form Neryon expects. That, I suspect, will be a greater shock to him than if he had not been forewarned.

He will be thrown completely off his guard, and a man off guard is a far easier target!'

Malia was silent for a few moments. Then, slowly, she too began to smile.

'Yes,' she said. 'Yes . . . I understand you, Thel. And I think you are right.'

'I know I am,' said Thel. 'Trust me, my dear Malia. I know.'

17

Shar, Hestor and Kitto spent a nerve-racking night behind the bolted door of the apartments. None of them slept for more than a few minutes at a time, and the smallest sound sent Hestor's hand flying to his sword-hilt and Kitto's to the handle of the knife he had taken from the castle kitchens. But nothing came to threaten them. If Lemor Carrick had a new move in mind, he wasn't yet ready to make it. Possibly he was waiting for instructions from Thel, or possibly he was simply biding his time. Either way, by the time a rainy dawn broke they had been plagued by nothing worse than sleeplessness and their own imaginations.

Which, Hestor told himself, seemed just a little too good to be true. If Shar was so vital to their plans, then surely the assassins would make every effort possible to snatch her back? Yet, apart from that one visit by Carrick, nothing had happened. That didn't ring right to Hestor. And it set him thinking.

With daylight, more visitors began to arrive at the castle; adepts from the provinces, parties of Sisters from various Cots and even a few dignitaries from the Margravate towns. As each new party clattered into the courtyard, Hestor or Kitto would dive to the window, dreading to see Thel and Malia among the arrivals. But they didn't appear. Shar ventured the hopeful thought that maybe her escape had forced them to abandon their plot after all.

Kitto was sceptical. 'They're bound to have another trick or two up their sleeves.'

Hestor looked up sharply at this last comment. Another trick up their sleeves . . . His unease at the lack of any further move from Carrick had been nagging at him all morning. There had to be a reason for this lull. And he thought he might just know what it was.

'Shar.' He stood up abruptly, startling both the others. 'Shar, listen. I don't want to scare you, but I've got a feeling – an intuition, if you like – that before you escaped from Thel, he might have done something to you.'

'Done something?' She looked back at him warily. 'What do you mean?'

'I'm not quite sure. But when Kitto said what he did about tricks, it made a horrible kind of sense.' He paused. 'When you were learning the ritual, did Thel ever put you under hypnosis?'

'No.' Shar shook her head, then frowned. 'Though if he did, would I know about it?'

'Exactly. Look, Shar, I know I'm only a first-rank initiate, but I think I've got enough magical skill to find out if there's something in your mind that you're not aware of.' He hesitated again, then asked, 'Do you trust me enough to let me try?'

Shar looked steadily back at him. 'Yes,' she said, 'I do.' Deep down she felt a surge of anger, of revulsion, as her loathing for Thel became a hard, tight knot inside her. 'Because if he has done something to me, I want to know what it is. And I want to wipe it out!'

Kitto sat hunched on the window seat in front of the closed curtains, his face white in the gloom as he watched Hestor and Shar. The castle was now a hive of activity, as more and yet more guests arrived, and Hestor knew that Carrick, like the other senior adepts, would be kept busy welcoming the visitors. He could safely assume that they wouldn't be interrupted, so he had fetched the magical items he needed from his mother's room and was ready to begin his work.

Shar sat on a chair in the middle of the room. She had felt the faint tremor that permeated the atmosphere as Hestor cast a protective astral barrier around them, and now she was staring into a small scrying-glass set on a table before her. The mirror reminded her unpleasantly of Thel's sorcery in the cellar of the retreat-house, but she tried not to think about that; tried instead to concentrate, as Hestor had asked, on the sweet and pleasant scent of the incense burning in a crucible between her and the glass.

Amber crouched on the floor at her side. He was utterly still but Shar could sense great unease emanating from his mind. Every now and then his green glance would flick briefly to Hestor, and once – as the mirror was put in place – he had uttered a soft growl. But he made no attempt to interfere.

Hestor moved quietly to stand behind Shar's chair, and laid his hands lightly on her shoulders. 'Look into the glass,' he said. 'Then try to look through it and beyond it.'

She obeyed, and through the veils of incense smoke saw her own face, pale and tense, staring back. With an effort she made her eyes unfocus; the image blurred and she seemed to see darkness behind the glass. Then a rainbow of colours appeared in the mirror. Pale green, sky blue, shimmering gold . . .

'Good,' Hestor said softly, and she knew that he, too, could see the rainbow. 'That's good . . . nothing amiss there.'

Shar wanted to ask what the colours meant, what they told him, but didn't dare speak lest her concentration should slip. She heard Hestor chanting under his breath, felt a tingle run through her blood as her consciousness seemed to slide to a deeper level, like swimming down into a well of water. The colours, too, started to deepen; dark green and midnight blue now, and the gold had a sunset tinge to it.

Then, so suddenly that she jolted in the chair, the gold flashed into hot, burnt orange, and with a violent flicker the rainbow changed; purple, blood red, a filthy brown. A suffocating sensation clutched at Shar's lungs, and Amber sprang to his feet with a furious snarl. The colours seemed to snake out of the mirror at her; she jerked backwards—

And the mirror turned utterly black for a single second before clearing to show nothing more than the reflections of the room.

'Kitto, open the curtains!' Hestor's voice brought Shar's mind whirling back to normal, and moments later the room was flooded with daylight. Kitto jumped from the window seat and ran to her. 'Shar! Shar, are you all right?'

'Yes, I – I'm fine.' She made to stand up, then thought better of it and subsided, shaking her head. 'Gods!'

Amber jumped on to Shar's lap, projecting anxious but muddled thoughts, and Shar stroked him to calm them both. 'What did it mean?' she asked.

'That I was right,' Hestor said. 'Thel has implanted something in your mind, and he must have hypnotised you to do it. There's no trace of anything in your consciousness, but as soon as the glass started to show the deeper layers we both saw it. The red and purple were a sure sign of something unpleasant.'

'You don't need to tell me that!' Shar said with feeling. 'Did I break the spell, Hestor? Did I spoil it?'

'When it suddenly flashed into black, you mean? No, that wasn't you. That was a barrier. Thel would have put it there to stop anyone probing any further.'

'I see.' She nodded gravely. 'Then, although we know now that there is some hypnotic command in my mind, we still don't know what it is.'

'No, but I can make a guess,' Hestor said tautly. 'It's a safeguard against any thought you might have of defying him.'

'He told me what would happen if I did . . .' Shar shivered.

'I know, but it seems he wasn't prepared to rely on that alone. I think he's found another way to force you to perform that ritual. If you do try to resist, he'll trigger that hypnotic command and you won't be able to stop yourself from doing what he wants.'

A cold, heavy, dead sensation seemed to settle in the pit of Shar's stomach at the thought of how helpless and vulnerable that made her. Her voice unsteady with bitter anger, she said, 'Can you break it. Hestor? *Can* you?'

'I wish to all the gods I could. But Thel's a skilled sorcerer; it would take a very high-ranking adept indeed to unravel what he's done.' Hestor sighed. 'In fact I think the High Initiate is the only one who can help us.'

They were quiet for a few moments. At last Shar said, 'Then we'll simply have to wait. We've no other choice, have we?'

'No,' said Hestor. 'We've no other choice.'

Kitto brought food for them all from the dining-hall, but no one felt like eating. Shortly after noon Shar fell into an exhausted sleep on Pellis's bed, attended by Amber, and the boys took turns to rest or keep watch at the window. But neither of them could manage more than a shallow, dream-haunted sleep. And still there was no sign of Thel.

The afternoon dragged drearily and uncomfortably by. Then, as dusk at last began to close in, the High Initiate and his companions emerged from the spire.

Shar was at the window when they appeared. She had slept for most of the afternoon, and when she woke had insisted that she too should take her turn in watching. She saw the spire door open, but for a few moments didn't think it particularly significant. Only when a group of people in the courtyard started to move towards the spire did she tense, suddenly alert – and then she saw Neryon Voss step outside, followed by Pellis and the other adepts who had kept vigil with him.

'Hestor!' Shar ran into the adjoining room where the boys were curled up on Pellis's wide bed. Weariness had got the better of dreams at last, and they were both soundly asleep. 'Hestor! Kitto! Wake up! The High Initiate has returned!'

Hestor's eyes snapped wide open. '*What*?'

'They all came out just a few moments ago,' Shar told him. 'They're in the courtyard!'

Hestor got up and ran to the window, with Kitto, now awake, stumbling behind him. Neryon Voss was moving towards the castle's main doors, but more and more people were gathering round him as word of his appearance spread rapidly.

Hestor groaned. 'Half the castle wants to see him – with all the visitors as well, the queue outside his study will stretch halfway to Chaun Province!'

'Barge them, then,' Kitto said. 'We can't afford to wait!'

Hestor's eyes narrowed. 'Maybe Mother would . . .' Then he stopped. 'No; you're right, there isn't time to do this politely. Kitto, find Mother, and bring her back here as quickly as you can. Shar, you'd best stay and wait for her.'

Shar wanted to act rather than wait, but she acknowledged that until the High Initiate had been alerted the risk couldn't be taken. She nodded. 'Be careful, both of you. If Carrick sees you . . .'

'There are too many people around for him to try anything.' Hestor headed for the door. 'Lock yourself in after we've gone.'

'I will. Good luck!'

Hestor and Kitto raced along the corridor and pounded down the main staircase. The entrance hall was crowded and people stared disapprovingly at their haste, but they ignored the frowns and divided off on their separate missions, forging their way through the throng. Hestor turned into the passage leading to the High Initiate's study, and to his dismay saw at once that it was even more crowded than the hall had been. Though most of those waiting wore adepts' badges, many of their faces were unfamiliar, and Hestor wondered, with a chill shiver, if any of these men and women were accomplices of Thel's.

He looked again at the size of the queue waiting to see Neryon and knew that there was only one thing to be done. Caution – and manners – must go to the four winds, and if trouble came about as a result, so be it. Taking a deep breath like a swimmer about to dive underwater, Hestor plunged into the crowd, jostling and fighting his way towards the study door. There were exclamations, protests of surprise and indignation; someone, forgetting himself, swore roundly at Hestor's impertinence, but Hestor pushed on, using shoulders and elbows to force his way through.

By a small miracle, no one actually stopped him. People were caught unawares by his sheer audacity, and by the time they had even thought about reacting he was past them and pressing on. One of the castle stewards was on duty outside the study; recognising Hestor he started to say, 'What do you think you're—' But Hestor ignored him. He reached out for the latch and, before the startled man could catch hold of him, flung the door open and stumbled over the threshold.

Neryon Voss was sitting at his desk, and there were four other people, all strangers, in the room with him. The High Initiate looked up in surprise as Hestor burst in, and his face contorted in fury.

'Hestor! What in the sacred names of the gods do you mean by this?'

'Sir, this is an emergency!' Breathless from his efforts, Hestor paused to drag air into his lungs. The others were staring at him, curiosity, censure and a small measure of amusement showing on their faces. Were they friends or enemies? Hestor had not the slightest idea, but there was no time now to be cautious. If he didn't tell the truth in the next few seconds, Neryon would throw him out.

'I'm sorry, sir. But it's Shar. She's here – and she's found out the whole truth! She's a Dark-Caller! And her uncle—'

'Wait.' Neryon cut across him with such forceful authority that he fell instantly silent. The High Initiate glanced from one to another of his visitors, then said, 'Ladies, gentlemen – I hope you'll forgive me, but it seems this is an extremely urgent matter. I need to speak to Hestor alone.' He looked towards the door, where the steward was hovering anxiously, and added, 'It's all right, Simik. I'll deal with this. Perhaps you'd be so kind as to escort my guests out, and offer my apologies to the others who are waiting.'

The guests were clearly a little piqued at being dismissed so abruptly, but they went, and Simik, agog with interest, reluctantly closed the door again.

'Now, Hestor.' Neryon had risen to his feet and was staring hard at the boy. 'What's this about Shar being a Dark-Caller? Tell me, quickly!'

Hestor did, and as he listened Neryon's expression grew dark.

'Great Gods . . .' He spoke very softly. 'And for all these years the Circle has been none the wiser . . . Where is Shar now?'

'In our apartments,' Hestor said. 'Kitto went to look for my mother.'

'He should have found her by now. Come with me and we'll join them.'

There was a rush of voices when they emerged from the study, as people pressed forward to greet the High Initiate and ask if anything was amiss. Neryon deftly fielded the questions, and with a few courteous but terse apologies steered Hestor away towards the main stairs.

Pellis had reached the apartments before them. She welcomed Hestor with a swift hug, but it was clear that her main concern was with Shar, who now sat beside Kitto on the couch. The High Initiate greeted Shar gravely, then turned to Pellis and said, 'It seems we have an extremely serious situation on our hands. Has Shar told you everything?'

'She's told me enough,' Pellis replied grimly. 'I believe her, Neryon.'

'So do I. However, I want to ensure that we have the facts absolutely right.' Neryon's glance swept over Shar, Hestor and Kitto. 'I want to hear the whole story again, in as much detail as possible. I'm sorry to ask this of you all, but even the smallest scraps of information may be vital.'

So the entire tale was repeated once more while Neryon listened intently, interrupting only twice to ask a question. At last the three had told him all they could, and for a few moments silence closed in on the room. Four pairs of eyes were focused on the High Initiate's face, and Neryon stared at his own steepled fingers, his expression unreadable. Then quietly and soberly, he said, 'If Lord Yandros himself has seen fit to guide us in this, there can be no possible shadow of doubt. And Shar's description of the ritual she has been taught is clear and final proof.' He looked up, and his gaze met Shar's. 'I know that ritual, although to my knowledge it hasn't been performed for more than a hundred years. And I believe I also know how and when Thel will make his bid to kill me. At the height of the ceremony tomorrow night, he'll publicly challenge me to prove my fitness to lead the Circle—'

Hestor's mouth opened in outrage and he interrupted. 'He can't do that!'

'Hestor!' Pellis said severely. But Neryon only gave Hestor a sour smile.

'If you'd paid a little more attention to your studies, Hestor, you'd know that he can. Any adept of the Circle is entitled to challenge the High Initiate's rule if he or she feels it right to do so. It's an old law, to safeguard the Circle against tyranny.'

Hestor looked abashed, and Shar asked, 'What will happen then, sir?'

'By tradition, the challenger and High Initiate confront each other in a sorcerous contest. That, of course, is when Thel intends to use you to summon the creature from the sixth plane. With the eclipse to give it strength, I won't have the power to control such a being. But Thel – again through you, Shar – will have that power. And the last words of the ritual you've learned will give the creature the command to destroy me.'

'Sir, you must arrest them!' Hestor said vehemently. 'Physician Carrick's already here in the castle, and Thel and Sister Malia are sure to arrive before long! Send armed men, and—'

'No, Hestor,' the High Initiate replied. 'That would only give us the ringleaders, and it isn't enough. I want to unmask all the plotters. If some evade capture they'll be free to plan another strategy, and that could put Shar in further danger, for they may try to use her again.'

Hestor hadn't thought of that, and he subsided. 'When Thel issues his challenge,' Neryon continued, 'that will be the moment for his co-conspirators to reveal themselves, for they'll stand with him to lend their magical strength. We must wait until then.'

'But sir, that's even more dangerous!' Hestor protested. 'If Thel has implanted a hypnotic command in Shar's mind, there won't be time to arrest him before he triggers it!'

'I'm well aware of that, Hestor,' Neryon said. 'But I'll have to take the risk.' He looked thoughtfully at Shar. 'Ideally I would have liked to nullify that spell, but there isn't time; without knowing exactly what Thel has done it could take several days to undo his work. However, if Thel does try to trigger it I should be able to protect Shar from the compulsion, provided she's close enough to me at the time. And that will be a simple matter. I'll take her as one of my cloak-bearers during the eclipse – and you, Hestor, can be the other.'

On great formal occasions where the High Initiate wore full ceremonial regalia, the train of his cloak was traditionally carried by two attendants chosen from the first rank of the Circle. Hestor had never before been offered that privilege, but the pride and excitement he should have felt was blotted out by dismay.

'But sir,' he said, 'Shar isn't a Circle initiate. She can't take part in the rite.'

'She isn't an initiate yet, I agree,' Neryon replied. 'But it's high time that oversight was remedied.' He looked at Shar once more, and smiled dryly. 'After all, there's only one proper place for someone who was born a Daughter of Storms and a Dark-Caller together. And that's under the guidance and protection of the Circle, as a trained adept.'

Shar realised what Neryon was saying to her, and her eyes widened. The High Initiate had given her the chance to fulfil her lifelong dream, and though that chance had come in unpleasant circumstances, it still sent a dizzying thrill through her.

'Well, Shar?' Neryon's voice was a little sterner now. 'Are you willing to undergo the rite, and take the oath of loyalty?'

She swallowed. 'Yes, sir,' she whispered. 'Oh, yes – I'm more than willing!'

18

'In the name of Yandros, highest lord of Chaos, and in the name of Aeoris, highest lord of Order, I charge these adepts who stand beside me to witness that Shar Tillmer is now, in her own right, an initiate of the Circle. Rise, initiate, and be welcome among us.'

Neryon Voss's solemn words echoed through the Marble Hall, and Shar, who knelt before him on the mosaic floor, raised her head as though in a dream. Neryon was smiling down at her; at his right hand Pellis was smiling too, and at his left Hestor was trying to maintain a serious expression and suppress an enormous grin.

Slowly, Shar rose to her feet. She was trembling, she could barely believe that this was happening. But the High Initiate was stepping forward to cast a brown cloak round her shoulders – brown was the colour of the Circle's first rank. Then, as she held her breath, he pinned the star and circle badge to her shoulder. Shar gazed steadily ahead, unblinking, though inwardly she wanted only to stare and stare at the badge. She ached with pride and with a happiness that even the present turmoil couldn't diminish. Her dream had come true. And in her heart she knew that, had they only lived to see this moment, her parents would have rejoiced for her.

Neryon stepped back again, and suddenly the atmosphere in the Hall changed. The initiation ceremony had been surprisingly short and, in many ways, unremarkable; simply a formality of words without any obvious magical significance. But all the same Shar had sensed an eerie background feeling in the air, a strange, unearthly thrill that seemed to carry a promise of its own. Simple though the ceremony was, she had felt that a greater power was listening and approving. Now, abruptly, that power had loosed its hold on the scene and withdrawn, and with its going everything seemed suddenly and almost disappointingly normal. Even the colours of the swirling mists were muted, and Pellis's footsteps as she ran to hug Shar broke the last of the thrall and brought her completely back down to earth.

'Welcome, my dear!' Pellis said warmly. 'I'm so pleased for you!'

Hestor, too, hugged Shar. Then Neryon spoke.

'I'm afraid there can be no celebration, such as we usually hold for a new candidate,' he said. 'But the main thing is done. As Pellis says, Shar, welcome.'

'Thank you, sir.' She almost made the obeisance the Sisters had taught her, then remembered in time and instead bowed in the manner of Circle initiates. Neryon's eyes showed approval, and he continued, 'Pellis will look after you from now on, and she will also instruct you and Hestor in the duties you must perform as my cloak-bearers tomorrow. There'll be little time to speak to you again before the eclipse ceremony begins, so I'll say now that I hope the gods will look kindly on us all. Goodnight.'

They watched him walk away. He looked, Shar thought, very, very tired. Then Pellis turned and smiled. 'Well, my dears, this has been a momentous night, and you must both be weary. Come along – remember, Kitto will want to hear everything before you have the chance to sleep!'

They were about to follow her out of the Hall when Shar hung back. 'Pellis . . . might I please have a few moments with Hestor before we leave? There's something I want to say to him.'

Pellis understood and nodded. 'Of course. I'll wait for you in the library.'

They stood silent until she had gone, then Hestor said, 'What is it you want to tell me?'

'I just wanted to say thank you.' Suddenly Shar felt awkward, but she had to get the words out; had to express what was in her mind. 'If it hadn't been for you, none of this could possibly have happened.'

Hestor smiled and gave a short little laugh to cover his embarrassment. 'What? Thel's treachery, and the assassination plot?'

'Ohh . . . You know perfectly well what I mean!'

Hestor tone sobered. 'Yes. Yes, I do.' The smile came back. 'I'm glad for you. Relieved, too, because at last you'll have the chance to learn to use your powers properly, and control them.' He nodded towards the door of the Marble Hall, invisible through the mists. 'Neryon means to undertake some of your training himself. I heard him saying so to Mother.'

Shar was surprised. 'But he's High Initiate! He surely won't trouble with a novice like me?'

'Oh, he will. Don't look so nervous. He's a superb teacher, and not as formidable as he seemed during the initiation ceremony.'

Shar smiled faintly. 'He did frighten me then. I sensed that he had tremendous power, and he seemed very intimidating and remote.'

'That's hardly surprising – after all, he is the gods' chosen representative.' Though after meeting Yandros face to face, Hestor thought privately, he doubted if he would ever be awed by a mere mortal again. Then his expression because pensive. 'Neryon is a powerful sorcerer, but tomorrow night he's going to be put to the greatest test he's ever faced. And I think he knows that even his abilities aren't enough. He's afraid, Shar.'

Shar stared into the shifting mists as the warm glow she felt in the wake of her initiation chilled suddenly into something darker. She, too, had seen Neryon's fear. And though pride and determination made her reluctant to admit it, even to Hestor, she shared that fear in huge measure.

'He said, "I hope the gods will look kindly on us all" ' she mused. 'Do you think they will, Hestor?'

Hestor recalled Yandros's face, and the careless words of the Chaos lord which had seemed to mask a deeper interest. But how could he predict what attitude Yandros would or wouldn't take? It was well known that gods, and the gods of Chaos in particular, were capricious.

Aloud, he said, 'I honestly don't know. Yandros sent the Warp that enabled you to escape, and I'm sure' – dared he assume this? He hoped so – 'that he must approve of your being initiated into the Circle. But he said that he won't intervene any further. It'll be up to Neryon, and you, to fight Thel.' He saw her expression and sighed. 'I'm sorry. But it's the truth.'

'I'd rather hear the truth.' It was preferable to a comfortable lie, Shar told herself . . . but nonetheless, a lie might have helped her to sleep better tonight.

'Come on,' Hestor said. 'We'd better not keep Mother waiting.'

They started to walk out of the Marble Hall. As they went, Shar looked back, once, to where the seven statues of the gods stood motionless and forbidding. The mists blurred detail, but she fancied that there was something very slightly different about the carved face of Yandros. As if the stone figure's mouth had curved in a faint, sardonic smile . . .

Hestor had walked on ahead. Shar suppressed a shudder, and ran to catch up with him.

Against the odds, Shar was so tired that she did sleep that night, and dreamlessly. But early in the morning she was woken by Amber, who jumped on to her pillow and pushed his face agitatedly against hers.

'Amber?' Shar opened her eyes, blinking blearily. 'What is it, what's the matter?'

The ginger cat miaowed, sprang down from the bed and ran to the window. He leaped on to the sill and stared out. Then he lashed his tail and hissed, and Shar sensed anger coming from his mind.

She pushed the blankets back and went to the window to join him. Down below, two new visitors had just ridden in and were dismounting in the courtyard. Their faces and clothes were all too familiar, and her heart gave a painful lurch. Thel and Malia had arrived.

A groom came to take the newcomers' horses, and Thel and Malia looked around them, as though searching for something – or someone. Shar moved back so that the curtain would hide her, and watched as they walked towards the main doors. As they started up the steps a figure emerged from inside the castle. It was Neryon. He, too, must have seen them arrive, and all three stopped and began to speak to each other. Shar wished fervently that she could hear what was being said, but glass and the distance made it impossible. She saw, though, that they were all smiling . . .

Amber made a little growl deep in his throat and it snapped Shar out of her trance. The three were going into the castle now, still talking, and she turned from the window and ran out of the room to find Hestor and Kitto.

'He certainly greeted us cordially enough,' Sister Malia said when at last she and Thel were alone. 'Yet Shar must have told him her story.'

'Of course she must,' Thel agreed. 'Whatever she knows, we can be sure that Neryon knows it too. But he also knows that he can't do anything until and unless our intentions are proved beyond any doubt.' He smiled. 'And by the time that happens, it will be too late.'

Malia nodded. 'So by this time tomorrow,' she said, 'the Circle will have a new High Initiate.'

'Indeed it will.' Once Neryon was dead, Thel knew, no one would question his right to step into Neryon's shoes. No one would dare question it, for any sorcerer who could command and control the powers of the sixth plane was a man to be feared.

'Neryon should never have been elected High Initiate in the first place,' he said with withering contempt. 'He was given the title simply because his ancestors have held it for generations, but he's not fit for such a high office! He's easy-going; he's weak – he doesn't make any worthwhile use whatever of his power! Believe me, Malia, when he is gone, the Circle will see some changes!'

Malia could feel the sting of his burning, jealous ambition; an ambition he had held ever since, as a young adept, he had realised that he would never be able to claim the High Initiate's role in his own right. Malia understood his feelings of resentment and envy, for she shared them. She remembered the promise Thel had made to her: that within a year of his taking power, she would become Matriarch of the Sisterhood. It wouldn't only be the Circle, she told herself contentedly, that would change. And no one would dare to oppose them.

'We must see Carrick,' Thel said, 'and make sure that everything is prepared.'

'And Shar?' Malia asked.

Thel smiled again. 'We've no need to worry about her. When the time comes, she'll do what needs to be done. She'll have no choice.'

Throughout the day, the atmosphere in the castle built up to a feverish pitch. Everyone was tense and excited, and the great old building was in turmoil as the final preparations for the eclipse ceremony were made.

Pellis had carefully schooled Shar and Hestor in the duties they must perform as the High Initiate's cloak-bearers. Their tasks were simple enough, but as she listened to Pellis's instructions Shar found it very hard to concentrate. She felt queasy, hadn't been able to eat a thing at breakfast or at lunch, and the dark shadows of her fears were closing in on her like predators. A terrifying list of 'what if's paraded ceaselessly through her mind, and she had the awful feeling that, at the last, she was going to lose her nerve and crumple. Hestor and Kitto both did their best to reassure her, but as the sun started to slip down the sky she felt she was in the grip of a nightmare from which there would be no awakening.

Dusk was closing in when Neryon came to see them all. He had time for only a brief visit, he said, for very soon he must go and make himself ready for the ceremony. But he spoke to them quietly of the danger they must face, and the need for great courage and determination, then he asked them to join him in the traditional evening prayers to the gods. They all made their devotions with especial passion; even Kitto, who had hardly ever prayed in his life, joined in fervently. Then Neryon left. But at the door, out of earshot of everyone else, he had a private word with Pellis.

'Pellis, I don't want to alarm the younger ones, so this is for your ears alone. I'm worried that if and when things start to go wrong for him, Thel will resort to desperate measures.'

Pellis nodded. She too had had the same feeling.

'He might well try to increase the power he's calling on,' Neryon continued. 'If he does that, he will of course use Shar, and if in the heat of the moment he makes one small slip, then the power might rebound on her. I don't need to tell you what that would mean.'

'It would kill her,' Pellis said softly. 'She wouldn't stand a chance.'

'Exactly. So I want to enlist your help. I want you to shadow Thel from the moment the ceremony begins. Watch his every move, be alert for the least sign of anything untoward.'

'He's sure to realise that I'm doing it,' said Pellis.

'I know. But the realisation might make him think twice before making any reckless move. For Shar's sake – and mine – I'd be grateful for your help in that.'

'Of course.' She smiled apprehensively. 'I hope we've done enough, Neryon.'

'We've done all we can,' Neryon replied. 'Even the gods couldn't ask more of us than that.'

19

As the first ethereal silver glow tinged the castle walls, a hush fell on the great crowd gathered in the courtyard. Shuffling feet were stilled, whispered conversations fell away into silence, and all eyes turned to the two moons rising slowly together against the huge, dark backdrop of the sky.

From where she and Hestor waited in the entrance hall, Shar thought that the courtyard looked like a scene from a strange dream. So many people – castle-dwellers, servants, visitors – and those who hadn't been able to find space outside were gathered at windows and in doorways, anxious to see every moment of the spectacle. Every lamp in the castle had been extinguished, and the moonlight drained all colour from the scene; everything was black and silver, and the crowd looked pale and ghostly in the gloom. The first and larger moon had cleared the castle wall now, and the second was following it, moving more swiftly. Soon, Shar knew, they would begin to merge, and that would be the cue for the ceremony to begin. She glanced at Hestor, who looked solemn and determined, then at the High

Initiate waiting a pace or two ahead of them. Neryon was magnificent but intimidating in his ceremonial garments; white trimmed with green, the colour of a seventh-rank adept, and a long cloak woven from threads of pure gold that swept the floor at his back. On his head he wore a golden circlet set with fourteen gems, and at his hip hung an ancient and massive broadsword with a jewelled hilt, the ritual weapon of many High Initiates before him. Shar looked at the expression on his shadowed face, then with a shiver returned her gaze to the courtyard. Thel, Malia and Carrick would be out there, with Pellis watching them from somewhere nearby. And Kitto, she knew, wouldn't be far away; he had promised to find a vantage point where he, too, could be alert for trouble.

Suddenly there was a soft rush of sound from the courtyard, as though many voices were sighing in awe and anticipation. Shar tensed – then moments later the single, clear note of a horn wound shimmeringly up from the battlements above the barbican arch. It was the signal they had been awaiting. The discs of the two moons were beginning to join together, and the time had come for the ritual to begin.

Hestor whispered, 'Now,' and he and Shar bent to lift the train of the High Initiate's cloak. Behind them fourteen more initiates, all dressed in white and each carrying an unlit flamboy, moved into line. Another adept had stepped forward, holding out a golden chalice that brimmed with a dark liquid; Neryon took the chalice, then Shar's heart and stomach gave a queasy lurch as, with slow dignity, the procession began to move towards the main doors.

The faces of Thel and Malia watched eagerly as the High Initiate and his entourage emerged on to the steps. Neryon's white clothing and gold cloak made him an unearthly figure, and a second sigh went up from the throng as every head turned to see him. Solemnly he descended the steps and moved towards his appointed place, and for several seconds Thel didn't even think to look at the two young initiates who walked soberly in his wake. They were just children, unimportant. But then he saw the boy's face. It was familiar . . .

His gaze slid sideways to where Pellis stood not two paces away. He knew perfectly well that she was shadowing him, but his smile was pleasant enough as he murmured, 'I see the High Initiate has chosen your son as one of his attendants, Pellis. You must be proud.'

'Indeed,' Pellis replied with an equally pleasant smile.

Wanting to maintain the pretence of friendship, Thel continued, 'I can't see the girl attendant clearly. Who is she?'

Pellis's smile broadened a little. 'Don't you recognise her, Thel?'

Thel looked harder; and suddenly Malia gripped his arm and made a strangled sound as the girl moved into a patch of moonlight. With her hair looped up and bound with a silver circlet she looked older, and Malia hadn't at first recognised her. But there could be no mistake. The second attendant was Shar. And pinned to the shoulder of her simple white robe with its brown sash was the gold badge of a Circle initiate.

'What . . .?' Thel took a ferocious grip on himself and swung to face Pellis again. 'What is this?' he demanded in a furious whisper.

Pellis looked serenely back at him. 'Shar returned to the castle a few days ago,' she said, as if Thel hadn't been aware of it. 'She was initiated last night, at Neryon's insistence. As a Daughter of Storms, he felt it only right that she should be brought into the Circle so that she can be properly trained.' She smiled again, sweetly but with a hard edge. 'We're all very pleased for her.'

Thel felt Malia grip his arm again, silently communicating alarm. He shook her hand off, moved a covert step away from Pellis, then said in a murmur that only Malia could hear, 'Be calm!'

'We hadn't anticipated this!' Malia hissed back. 'Neryon Voss is planning something! He must be!'

'Even if he is, it makes no difference. I haven't come this far only to turn coward and back out at the last moment! Besides, a mere initiation ceremony means nothing. Neryon might think it will protect her, but he'll soon find out that he's wrong. When—'

Malia nudged him suddenly. 'Best say nothing more. Pellis is still watching us.'

'Ah, Pellis . . . yes, she is a nuisance.' Thel gazed around the sea of faces, then saw Carrick a short way off. The physician caught his eye; Thel glanced expressively in Pellis's direction and Carrick gave the slightest of nods.

Thel was satisfied. Carrick understood his meaning; understood what was required. If Pellis was part of a trap that Neryon thought to set, then that trap would not be sprung. Carrick would see to it.

He turned, his face composed, to watch the ceremony once more.

The Circle's chant began as the two moons began to slide together and merge, and the sound of it sent a quivering thrill through Shar's bones. It started as a deep, slow cadence of male adepts' voices, then the higher, purer tones of the women joined in, creating a strange harmony that was almost but not quite discordant. The massed voices rose into the night like the surging of the sea, and the atmosphere in the courtyard grew electric as the Circle's will and purpose became one. They were focusing their minds, summoning power, and Shar's skin tingled as though she were standing on a hilltop in the breathtaking minutes before the breaking of a storm. She wanted to look at Hestor, but the thrall of the chant held her attention riveted on the moons as they drew closer, closer . . .

At the moment when the two shining faces fused and became one, the chant swelled into a single, stirring chord, and stopped. In the awed silence that followed, Neryon raised his arms high, the chalice held in both hands. The moons' united glare lit the chalice and turned it to searing brilliance, and in a rich, compelling tone Neryon began to speak the ritual exhortation to his fellow adepts. He called on them to use their sorcerous arts to protect the world while the gods' eyes could no longer see, and the adepts answered him in eldritch chorus. Energy was building up in the courtyard; the air seemed to crackle with it, and at the summits of the four spires an eerie glow reflected like ghostly fire.

The High Initiate chanted, the adepts responded . . . and gradually a dark shadow began to move over the faces of the moons. The eclipse was beginning. Hestor, standing beside Shar, stole a glance in her direction and saw her staring at the creeping darkness in the sky. She was mesmerised by the sight and by the ceremony, and he reminded himself that this was her first experience of a powerful Circle rite. It would be all too easy for her to lose herself in it and forget to be alert for danger, and Hestor suppressed a shiver at the thought. The ritual was nearing its height now, and the air seemed to pulsate as the adepts raised more and more magical energy. The shining disc in the sky was being steadily covered, as though some vast, dark and spectral creature were slowly devouring it. Shadows loomed and stretched menacingly from the walls, and then, stunningly, the last sliver of cold fire in the heavens vanished, and where the moons had been hung a perfect black circle, surrounded by a dim and phantasmic silver glow. The courtyard plunged into darkness. The eclipse was complete.

For a moment, absolute silence reigned. Neryon stood motionless, still holding up the chalice. Then, with an abrupt movement, he upturned it, so that its contents spilled to the ground. And at that signal, light flooded out from the castle battlements as seven times seven torches were ignited and flared into blazing life.

In the hot glare Hestor saw the High Initiate fling a rapid glance over his shoulder to the place in the throng where he knew Thel was standing. His stomach seemed to turn over, for he knew – as did Neryon – that this was the perfect moment for Thel to make his move. But it did not come. The crowd waited, silent and still, and though Hestor tried to glimpse Thel's figure, the dancing shadows cast by the torchlight made it impossible.

What was Thel doing? They had all been certain that he would choose this moment, at the climax of the ritual, to step out and issue his challenge to Neryon. Had something gone wrong? Hestor asked himself eagerly. Could it be that the plotters had lost their nerve at the last moment? He looked at Neryon again and saw that he was frowning. But the ritual must continue, and after a few moments the High Initiate drew breath to lead the adepts in a new chant, to strengthen the protective power that they had raised.

In the crowd, Pellis was watching Thel and didn't see the steward who was fighting his way through it towards her. Only when the man touched her shoulder respectfully did she start and turn.

'I beg your pardon, madam,' the steward said in a hoarse whisper, 'but it's the boy – the black-haired boy.'

'Kitto? Is something wrong?'

'An accident, madam. Apparently he had climbed up on to the stable roof for a better view, and he slipped and fell. Someone said that you have some concern with his welfare, and I was asked to bring word to you.'

'Dear gods!' Pellis's face grew worried. 'Is he badly hurt?'

'I don't know, madam. I think he might be. Should I send for Physician Carrick?'

Pellis could imagine what Carrick would do to Kitto if he had the chance, and she said, 'No, I'll come myself. Where is he?'

'By the stables, madam. We thought it better not to move him.'

From where he sat wedged precariously on a window ledge near the main doors, Kitto saw Pellis move away towards the edge of the crowd. He saw the steward staring after her, saw the sly smile on the man's face, and instantly his suspicions rose. What was going on? Was this some trick on Thel's part? Quickly he scanned the area and after a few moments glimpsed Thel. He, too, was smiling – but he was looking at Shar. And as Kitto watched, he raised one hand and his fingers traced a symbol in the air. . .

Hestor saw Shar sway suddenly on her feet, and in alarm he stage-whispered to her. 'Shar! Are you all right?'

'Y . . . yes,' Shar whispered back. 'I just felt dizzy for a moment.' But even as she said it, she knew in her bones that there was more to it than that. She had felt a violent impact in her mind, as though someone had struck her a psychic blow, and now her head seemed light and her limbs unsteady and remote, as though they belonged to someone else. Fight it, she told herself savagely. It's just your imagination. Fight it!

But it wasn't imagination, for suddenly the attack came again, and this time it took such a grip on her that she couldn't draw breath to warn anyone. Waves of giddy sickness flowed over her, making her feverishly hot and ice-cold by turns. And a voice seemed to be speaking in her head; a voice that commanded her to obey . . . obey . . . obey.

Hestor, thinking that perhaps the strain of the ritual was telling on her, reached out to steady her arm. With a sound like a snarl she threw him off and staggered sideways out of his reach. Then he saw her face, the terror in her eyes, and abruptly he knew the truth.

'Shar!' He reached towards her, and his shout of alarm stopped the High Initiate in his tracks. Neryon swung round. And the compulsion in Shar's mind swelled like a star bursting inside her skull.

'*No*!' Suddenly, shockingly, she screamed out, her voice echoing across the courtyard. 'I won't do it – *I won't*!'

Hestor tried to grab her as she swayed like a toppling tree, but she pushed him away with such ferocity that he stumbled backwards and almost fell. Regaining his balance he started towards her again, but a shout from Neryon stopped him.

'No, Hestor! Don't touch her!' The High Initiate's gaze was fixed on Shar's face, and inwardly he cursed himself for a fool. This had been Thel's plan all along – not to issue a formal challenge, but to attack without any warning whatever! He had triggered the hypnotic command in Shar's mind, and she was completely under his control!

Shar made an awful gagging noise, and her hands flew to her own throat as though she were trying to choke something back. She was struggling with all the willpower she possessed, but the spell Thel had cast on her was stronger, and Neryon knew she was losing the battle. There was only one chance, and though it would endanger her, he had to take it. He raised one arm and drew breath to call out the first words of a counter-spell.

Shar screamed in pain, and a weird, flickering aura sprang into life around her. Neryon recoiled in dismay as he recognised it – it was what the Circle called a protection-geas, a barrier against outside sorcery. And if anyone attempted to break it, the results could be lethal.

The courtyard was in disarray now as more and people realised that something had gone wrong with the ceremony. Voices began to rise in alarm and query, and some of the senior adepts were trying to leave their places and reach Neryon. But suddenly the growing hubbub was stilled as one single voice cut clearly and loudly through the disorder.

'Take your own advice to the boy, Neryon, and don't touch her. You know what will happen to her if you do.'

Shar moaned, and Thel stepped forward out of the crowd. His mouth was curved in a cold, cruel smile beneath his arctic-cold eyes.

'Yes, I have augmented the spell I placed on her,' he said, his words carrying to every ear in the stunned throng. 'And if you or anyone else tries to break the protection-geas, the power of it will rebound on her and kill her. For all your weakness, High Initiate' – he gave the title a note of bitter contempt – 'I don't think you are quite such a coward as to do that!'

Neryon's mouth set in a ferocious line and he pointed a finger at Thel. 'Thel Starnor, I arrest you as a traitor! Guards! Take him!'

From the edge of the courtyard armed men started forward. But Thel held up a warning hand.

'Make one move against me, and Shar will die,' he said. 'For I will turn the spell's power against her myself.' His gaze met Neryon's again. 'Don't think for one moment that I wouldn't do it, Neryon. One child's life means nothing to me!'

Neryon couldn't tell whether or not Thel was bluffing, but he knew he couldn't take the risk. Thel saw what he was thinking, saw the defeat in his face, and he smiled another, even colder smile.

'Shar.' He pivoted on one heel, and Shar found herself compelled to look at him. 'Speak the ritual I have taught you. Speak it now.'

Shar fought him. She fought him with every last fraction of strength she could dredge from her mind . . . but it wasn't enough. Whatever special power she might have locked inside her, she hadn't the knowledge or the training to use it against him. She could only obey, and, as though trapped in the throes of a monstrous nightmare, she heard her own voice rising shrilly as she began to cry out the words that would summon the horror from the sixth plane.

An abominable darkness began to boil in her mind. She knew where it came from – not from within herself but from another hideous dimension, and with each word of the ritual it grew stronger, eclipsing her will just as the two moons had been eclipsed. Through the dark fog of the aura around her she looked desperately, pleadingly, at Neryon and Hestor. But they were as helpless as she was. Everyone was helpless. No power in the world could come to her aid. There was only the madness inside her, and the inexorable ritual, and the horror of what was about to happen, what was about to break through the barrier between dimensions.

Her voice rang out, shrieking now, as the darkness in her head became greater and greater. The ritual was almost complete; she had one last hope, one last chance to drag herself back from the brink, and she shut her eyes, frantically fighting, *fighting* . . .

Pain blazed in her skull and the power of Thel's sorcery swamped her. She heard herself call out the last twisted words of the summoning spell, and in the same moment her aura blazed violently, like silver fire. Then, shocking everyone in the courtyard, silence crashed down.

The silence lasted for perhaps five, perhaps ten seconds. And then from the dark mouth of the barbican arch came a hideous, unhuman laugh.

Shar felt her eyes opening. She didn't want to look. She didn't want to see it. But the power controlling her told her that she must, and she was forced to submit.

Like the wing of some monstrous thing of nightmare, a vast black shadow was rising from the gateway. It towered towards the sky, blotting out the castle wall behind it, and Shar moaned in horror, clapping her hands to her head as she saw what the shadow contained. It was worse, far worse, than anything she had seen in the mirror in the cellar room. It was an abomination, a travesty, a thing of seething greed and hatred . . . and *power*.

From the middle of the crowd someone screamed on a shrill, terrified note. And Thel cried out, his voice warped with triumph:

'There High Initiate! This is my challenge to you! Meet it and conquer it – *if you can*!'

20

Neryon stared at the shadow, which was now spreading like oily smoke above the courtyard, and knew in that moment that he was utterly alone. He could not call on the gods for help; they would not hear him. And he would not turn to his fellow adepts, for this was not their battle. The sixth-plane entity had no interest in them; he was its intended victim, and it would harm no one else – provided they stayed clear. Neryon knew that, if he let them, the Circle's adepts would be ready to give their lives to help him. But he would not allow them to make that sacrifice. He must face this alone.

And unless a miracle happened, he was going to die.

The appalling laughter rang out a second time, and the darkness began to coalesce and become more solid. The spectators in the courtyard were held in a thrall of terror, but some of the adepts, made of sterner stuff, were running to Neryon's side. Neryon saw them and yelled, 'No! Stay back from me! Clear the courtyard and get people into the castle. *That is an order!*'

They hesitated, torn between obedience and fear for their High Initiate's safety. But moans of fear were quavering from the throng; people were beginning to panic, and the adepts realised that they must be controlled or there would be mayhem. They peeled away from Neryon and started to direct the crowd towards safety. As the first of them jostled through the main doors, Neryon saw Thel standing alone in a clear space. One arm was pointing at Shar and his lips were moving in the words of an incantation. And the horror in the courtyard was growing taller, rising, spreading . . .

Shar had fallen to her knees, still clutching her skull and rocking back and forth now as she strove to break free of Thel's hypnotic hold. But her desperate efforts were useless, for the sixth-plane horror was filling her mind. Its hungry power was like a battering assault on her senses; yet somehow she was controlling and directing it. Pain surged through her in shuddering waves; she knew what Thel was forcing her to do, but she couldn't break free and stop the insanity in her head. Dimly, through a fog of shock and agony, she saw Neryon move past her and start to advance towards the entity, his head high and eyes blazing with determination. She knew that he was going to face it and try to defeat it, and she wanted to scream to him, *No! No!* But she couldn't bite back the other words, the words Thel was forcing her to say to keep the ravening monstrosity under his control. She could do *nothing*.

Suddenly, from the milling crowd, two figures erupted and came running towards her. Hestor had been among a press of adepts who had backed away at Neryon's order, while Kitto had sprung down from his ledge and forged his way against the tide retreating into the castle. Seeing them, one of the adepts shouted, 'Don't touch her – you'll only make matters worse!'

'How could they be worse?' Hestor yelled back. He and Kitto reached Shar together and grasped hold of her, hugging her and shaking her by turns in a frantic attempt to snap her out of the thrall. But within seconds they knew it was hopeless.

'She needs – more powerful friends – than us!' Kitto gasped distraughtly.

More powerful friends . . . The idea hit Hestor like a starburst and he cursed himself for a blind, stupid fool not to have thought of it before. Rounding on Kitto, he bawled, 'Cats!'

'What?'

'*Cats*! Get the castle cats – as many as you can! Hurry, Kitto, *hurry*!'

Kitto didn't understand, but the frenzy in Hestor's tone galvanised him. He turned and plunged back into the crowd, kicking and elbowing his way towards the main doors. Hestor paused only a moment to watch him go, then turned his attention to Shar again. Thel was taking no notice of them now; contemptuous of Hestor's efforts and confident that Shar was completely in his thrall, he was watching Neryon's slow progress across the courtyard, and relishing the

High Initiate's terror. And as its human victim drew nearer, the entity began to laugh again, the terrible sound echoing between the castle walls.

Hestor knew he had only minutes at most. Frantically he started to shout another kind of summoning spell, striving to call up the lower elementals, Shar's friends. He had no idea what they might be able to do; he was clutching at a wild chance. But even as he cried out he realised that the spell wasn't powerful enough. He was only a first-rank initiate; he didn't have the skill for this!

Several other adepts saw what he was doing and one ran towards him with a warning shout. 'Hestor, don't meddle!' He grabbed Hestor's arm, trying to pull him away, but Hestor fought him off.

'No! Help me summon elementals, any elementals, as many as you can! They love Shar, they'll help her!'

The adept started to argue, but suddenly a new voice joined in and Pellis, still breathless from her wild-goose chase, appeared beside them.

'Hestor's right!' she cried. 'The elementals might have the power to break through to Shar. We've nothing to lose by trying!' And, flinging her arms out, she started to chant the words of a more powerful summoning.

Kitto, battling back through the main doors with a struggling, spitting cat under each arm, emerged into the courtyard in time to see what looked like a small but ferocious storm explode into being above Shar's head. The lower elementals had come in answer to Pellis's call, and they swarmed whirling around Shar and Hestor, screeching alarm and fury.

Kitto swung round and yelled to the three servants who, too stunned to ask questions, had helped him gather more cats. They all dropped their burdens, and the cats, tails bristling, shot away down the steps, racing towards Shar. She was glassy-eyed now, blind to everything around her and rocking wildly back and forth. Words choked from her lips, alien words – she could no longer fight, she was lost, lost . . .

As the cats streamed to her, Hestor dropped to his knees and pounced on the first animal he could reach. He swung it forcibly to face him, locking his gaze with its own, and with all his willpower tried to project a telepathic message: Help her! Break the spell! Break the spell!

The cat understood and its yowl was answered by the others as it passed the message on. Hestor released it, and in an instant every cat froze, staring intently at Shar's face. Suddenly the words Shar was chanting faltered, and on the far side of the courtyard a vast shiver seemed to ripple through the dark horror towering into the sky. Hestor saw it, saw Thel realise, saw him turn in rage.

'Attack him!' Hestor yelled to the elementals. 'He's the one who hurt Shar. Attack him!'

The elementals responded. There was a shriek of air that went ear-splittingly up the scale, a rush of heat and cold, and a noise like boulders rolling down a mountainside. The entire swarm launched themselves at Thel and he vanished in the midst of a savage miniature tornado. Hestor shouted in jubilation – but an instant later his delight shattered as a power-bolt hurled from another part of the courtyard and smashed into the elementals' midst. *Carrick* – he was counter-attacking, and now two other adepts had hurled aside any pretence of secrecy and were joining him, driving the elementals back. With shrill, angry cries the creatures scattered, and Thel spun to face Shar. His face twisted with malevolent fury, he raised one arm and shouted a word in a high-pitched voice. Shar's flailing mind seemed to turn upside-down inside her skull as the power of the Dark-Caller surged in her, and a renewed gale of unhuman laughter dinned in her ears. The vast black shadow of the sixth-plane entity boiled overhead, seeming to suck the light of the torches into itself, then Shar's voice soared into a scream of pure terror as the full power of the sixth-plane being crashed into her mind. Dwarfing the unearthly apparition of the eclipse, the column of darkness rose like a gargantuan serpent, drawing itself up to rear above the High Initiate, above the castle, above them all. Just one word of the ritual remained – and when that word was spoken, the final barrier would shatter. The entity would strike. And in a single, devastating moment it would annihilate Neryon.

Hestor and Kitto, holding tightly to Shar but knowing she was beyond their reach, felt despair fill them as they stared transfixed at the immense phantasm. The cats had failed, the elementals had failed – there was nothing more they could do!

Then suddenly Kitto released Shar and clutched at Hestor's arm. 'Look!' he shouted, pointing. 'Behind it – the gods' eyes are opening!'

Like a pale fire flickering and dying, the aura around the moons had vanished, and in its place a thin crescent of furious silver light had appeared at one edge of the disc.

'Shar!' Hestor screamed. 'Shar, the eclipse is ending!' He shook her so violently that her head jolted back, and the shock of his action broke through the tumult in her mind. Ending . . . Moonlight . . . The eyes of the gods . . . From somewhere so deep inside her that she could barely grasp at it, a spark of fury awoke. Thel was about to triumph. She would not let it happen. Whatever the danger and the cost to herself, she would not let it happen!

The final word of the ritual was forcing itself into her throat, and Thel's willpower beat against hers like a storm-tide, compelling her to 'speak it, speak it, speak it'. Her mouth opened, her tongue moved – and with an effort that she felt must tear her apart, Shar made herself turn and twist the word into something else.

'Yand . . .' Her voice shuddered and cracked. 'Yan . . . dros! YANDROS!'

The entity's cacophonous laughter changed suddenly to a roar of insane hatred. The great shadow swayed, turned – and as Thel and Carrick cried out in wrath, the writhing horror twisted in on itself and started to spear down at Shar. Kitto yelled out in terror, but Hestor had heard Shar's defiant cry and without pausing to think he, too, shouted Yandros's name with all the power his lungs could muster. He heard Neryon's voice echoing his, and all the cats raised their heads and yowled in eerie chorus. The clamour clashed with the entity's roaring, and the next instant there was a *crack* so titanic that the castle shook to its foundations. Hestor was hurled off his feet and went sprawling on the flagstones; for a few wild moments he scrabbled blindly in darkness, then his senses came back and he raised his head dizzily.

Every torch had gone out and only the emerging moons lit the scene. The castle was absolutely silent, and every face was turned to the sky in amazement. For, in the midst of its deadly attack, the dark entity had frozen in midair. Neryon, a lonely figure in the centre of the courtyard, stood staring bewilderedly, and even Thel and Carrick were too shocked to make any move.

Then by the central fountain a quiet sound, almost like the rustle of a cloak, broke the silence. A shadow moved . . . and Hestor's eyes widened as Yandros stepped out of the gloom.

There was nothing at all dramatic about his arrival, but the instant he appeared, every head in the courtyard turned in renewed shock. For perhaps three seconds a paralysis held them and the scene was a tableau. The lord of Chaos said nothing, but as his ever-changing eyes raked the crowd, Hestor could feel the sheer supernatural energy that emanated from him.

Then Yandros glanced up at the towering but motionless sixth-plane creature and said calmly, 'You like to think that you have power because you owe the gods no allegiance. But to us, you and your kind are nothing.' Almost carelessly, he snapped his fingers. There was an awful noise from the entity; a moaning whimper that echoed dismally to the heavens. Then, like a candle being snuffed out, it vanished from the mortal world.

No human in the courtyard dared to move a muscle. They all knew, now, who the golden-haired man must be, and their gazes were fixed rigidly on him. Then, just as Hestor thought the tension would suffocate him, a cat's voice rose up in a long, plaintive wail, and Amber ran to where Shar sprawled on the flagstones. The little animal's action snapped the thrall; Neryon shook his head as though coming out of a trance, and in full view of everyone he dropped to one knee before Yandros and bowed his head.

'My lord!' His voice was reverent and heartfelt. 'You are a thousand times welcome – and you have my lifelong gratitude!'

'Rise, High Initiate,' Yandros said serenely. 'And give your thanks to the one – or rather the ones – who deserve them.' His eyes, a warm gold, focused on Shar, who was being helped to her feet by

Hestor, Kitto, Pellis and several other adepts, while the cats mewed around her. 'In refusing to speak that last word, Shar risked sacrificing her own life. You are in her debt, not mine.'

He walked towards Shar, and as he approached her she tried to kneel again. But Yandros shook his head.

'Must I tell everyone that there is no need to cower before me?' he said with mock severity, then smiled as he saw Shar begin to tremble. 'What you did tonight, Shar, was an act of high courage, and that is something the gods value greatly.'

Shar stared at the ground. 'You granted me the strength to do it, lord Yandros.'

'I?' To her surprise Yandros laughed. 'Oh no. The strength was your own. Yours, and the cats whose telepathic powers helped you to fight the hypnotic spell. I had no hand in it, for I and my brothers do not interfere in mortal affairs.'

Hestor said, 'But this was a mortal affair, my lord. And when we called to you, you answered.'

Yandros gave him a long, shrewd look. 'Yes, I answered. But only to remove a troublesome creature from a place where it had no business to be. That, in my opinion, is not intervention.'

Hestor opened his mouth again, but abruptly stopped as he saw Yandros raise a warning eyebrow. Swallowing, he felt himself break out in a cold sweat as he realised how close he had come to overstepping the bounds. The truth was, it *had* been intervention, and they both knew it. But if Yandros chose to pretend otherwise, who was he, Hestor asked himself, to argue? The gods of Chaos were wayward and unpredictable, and if they chose, on a whim, to bend the rules which they themselves had set so long ago, the only wise thing to do was keep silent and be eternally grateful.

He made a bow and said, 'Of course, my lord. As you say.'

During the last few minutes everyone's attention had been so fixed on Yandros that Thel and his co-conspirators were forgotten. Suddenly, though, Amber hissed, arched his back, and stared across the courtyard. An instant later a formation of elementals appeared, whirling agitatedly in the air by the stable block. With triumphant shrieks they dived, and there was a commotion as, belatedly, the humans realised what was afoot. Carrick and Sister Malia were making for the stables, helping Thel who was stunned and broken by the shock of seeing victory snatched from his grasp. All three tried to protect themselves from the attacking creatures; Carrick started to shout a spell, but Neryon's voice eclipsed his, roaring out an order, and armed men ran from the crowd.

Within a minute the escape bid was ended, and the shaken trio were brought to stand before Neryon. Sister Malia was crying, Carrick refused to meet the High Initiate's gaze. Only Thel stared coldly, bitterly, at the man he had hoped to overthrow. But he said nothing. There was nothing to say.

Neryon looked at them all, then sighed and turned to Yandros. 'My lord,' he said, 'if you will see fit to deliver justice—'

'No, High Initiate.' Yandros held up a hand. 'That is for you to do. Mortal crimes must be judged by mortals. Decide as you see fit.' Then his look became baleful. 'But I would suggest that you get them out of my sight, before I'm tempted to change my mind.'

With a close, hard-eyed knot of adepts guarding them, the three were hustled away into the castle. Neryon watched them go, and his face creased in a frown. 'We have all the ringleaders,' he said. 'But the identities of the rest are still unknown.'

'Are they?' Yandros smiled. 'I think not.' He looked down at the cats and they all came purring towards him. Then he nodded to where the elementals were perfoming a dance of celebration and victory in midair above the courtyard. 'Shar should ask her friends. They are wiser than most humans; they will know the guilty ones.'

Surprised, Neryon said, 'Shar . . .?' She met his gaze bemusedly, then realised what Yandros had meant.

'Little ones . . .' Her voice was soft and unsteady. But the elementals heard her and stopped still, hovering. Then her voice rang clear and strong across the courtyard. 'Who are they, little ones? Show me – show me them all!'

The elementals erupted into a spinning mass. Then the mass broke apart and five groups darted to hover, whistling and shrieking, over the heads of two senior adepts, a steward and two lesser servants.

The arrests were made quickly and without a struggle, and Neryon's eyes were cold with contempt as he watched the culprits being led away. Yandros, at his side, reached out and touched his shoulder lightly. Neryon started at the touch, then shivered and looked at the lord of Chaos.

'It's over, High Initiate,' Yandros said. 'I will leave you now . . . but before I go, I want to speak privately with Shar and Hestor.' His eyes turned crimson and he added, 'You owe them a great deal, Neryon.'

'I know it, my lord. And I will never forget.'

Neryon stepped back out of earshot as Yandros approached the two young initiates once more. Shar moved close to Hestor, still afraid to look at the god directly. But Yandros gently touched her chin and tilted her head up. To her surprise, her fear subsided and she managed to smile at him.

'You are a very special mortal, Shar Tillmer,' Yandros said, 'and your powers are rare. If you use them fully and wisely – and the Circle will guide you well in that – then I think you have an outstanding future to look forward to. And I will watch your progress with interest.'

Quaking, Shar stammered, "Th-thank you, lord Yandros.'

Yandros nodded, then glanced at Hestor, and to his surprise Hestor saw great amusement in his expression. 'I should direct you to look after her, Hestor,' he said.

'But I suspect she is more than capable of looking after herself. Would you agree?'

The corners of Hestor's mouth twitched. 'Yes, my lord,' he replied. 'I would.'

There were no more farewells to be made. Yandros simply turned on his heel, walked to the centre of the courtyard and, with a final courteous nod to the High Initiate, stepped into the shadows of the fountain. There was a slight rustle like the sound that had heralded his arrival, and then he was gone.

In the wake of his departure, the courtyard seemed suddenly, eerily quiet. The adepts were melting away, moving through the main doors and into the castle, and at last only the small group of Neryon, Hestor, Shar, Kitto and Pellis were left.

Shar looked up at the sky where the two moons were now moving apart. The shadow of the eclipse had gone. And the shadow of the horror from the sixth plane was nothing more than a dreamlike memory. She felt Hestor and Kitto move up beside her, and when they each took one of her hands and squeezed it wordlessly, she felt a sense of warmth kindle in her.

Then Neryon spoke.

'There is a great deal to be done in the wake of this,' he said gravely. 'In the morning I will want to have a long talk with you all . . . but now it's late, and the best remedy for what you have endured tonight is sleep. Go to your beds, and I'll see you tomorrow.'

Shar was still gazing at the sky. 'I don't want to go to bed yet,' she told Neryon. 'I don't think I could sleep. I'd like to stay out here for a little while longer.'

As if to add their own emphasis to her words, a group of elementals materialised from nowhere and flittered around the High Initiate's head. They scolded him, darting at his hair, and with a frown Neryon looked up at them.

'Cease!' he rebuked them. The elementals spiralled away, and Neryon turned his attention to Shar again.

'Initiate Shar,' he said sternly, 'there are two lessons that a new member of the Circle should learn from the very beginning. One is to keep some kind of control over creatures like that, however friendly they might be. And the other is that, when the High Initiate gives an order, he expects it to be obeyed.'

Shar's eyes widened in chagrin. But then she saw that, for all his fierce tone, Neryon's mouth was twitching as he tried to suppress laughter.

Suddenly the spark of warmth she felt flowered and filled her. As Yandros had said, it was over. She had nothing more to fear now, and no need to brood. She couldn't change the past, but the evil Thel had done, to herself, to her parents, to them all, had been avenged. And the future lay ahead of her. A future of promise.

Very carefully, Shar made the formal bow of a Circle adept, and said meekly, 'Yes, High Initiate.'